WILD WEST

TYSON WILD BOOK SIXTY

TRIPP ELLIS

TRIPP ELLIS

"He can't catch us?" JD said. "Can he?"

A few pillowy clouds hung in the azure sky. The brilliant sun blazed down, baking the asphalt. The two-lane blacktop stretched as far as the eye could see. A straight line that rose and fell with the undulating terrain, nestled amid the Texas Hill Country.

We were deep in the thick of it.

The sticks.

Cow country.

The landscape blurred by as we sped down the highway. Barbed wire fences enclosed large tracts of land. Cows lay in the shade while others grazed on patches of grass. Cacti and mesquite trees dotted the landscape. Iguanas sunned themselves on rocks. Rattlesnakes slithered on trails. Jackrabbits darted about, and don't get me started on the scorpions.

It was hot.

Unseasonably warm for November. The hottest on record in this region. You could fry an egg on the highway or the hood of your car if it was in the sun long enough. Even with air conditioning, you started to sweat in places you didn't want to. In August, the Texas sun could give the devil heat stroke. It would make hell seem like an oasis. This wasn't August, but damn, it felt like it.

The engine howled as the tachometer approached the redline. We were well into the triple digits. And why the hell not? There was nobody as far as the eye could see.

Except for the problem behind us.

I glanced at the side view mirror. "The lights are on. He's just pulling out."

It wasn't long before the red and blues flickered behind us.

We had blazed past a county sheriff, going fast enough to peel the paint from his car.

We were in a GT Metallic Silver base model 911 Carrera. Nothing extremely fancy by Porsche standards, but a supercar in its own right. Zero to 60 in 3.8 seconds and a top speed of 182 miles an hour. Plenty fast enough. Though it was a crime that it didn't come with a limited-slip differential. You had to bump up to the S model to get that. A feature you would really only notice on the track or in wet weather.

"Do you think the badge will get me out of this one?" JD asked. "I mean, would you give another cop a ticket?"

"Depends on how much of an asshole that cop was."

"I'm not an asshole," JD said with confidence.

"He might not see it that way," I said, pointing my thumb behind us.

Texas was known for a lot of things. Wide open spaces, guns, cattle, cheerleaders, football, and hard-ass small-town cops that just love to write tickets. Porsche tickets were a special treat. Under normal circumstances, we were going fast enough to be put underneath the jail. Reckless driving and a host of other infractions. At this speed, it might be more than just a ticket. It might be a night in jail.

I was reasonably certain, with a flash of the badge and an apologetic, deferential tone, that we might get out of this scenario with a stern lecture and maybe a small ticket.

But JD took that option off the table. "He can't catch us," he said with confidence as he stood on the accelerator.

The flat-six howled, and the Porsche blazed ahead.

I'm pretty sure we got close to the top speed.

The flashing lights in the side view mirror grew small, then disappeared completely as we crested a hill and dipped into the valley beyond.

JD looked over at me and grinned.

I didn't share his enthusiasm.

The car was a rental. We'd picked it up in Austin after we'd hopped on the next plane out of Coconut Key. An urgent call from the daughter of an old friend brought us here. She was in dire straits and didn't know where else to turn.

The front trunk was big enough for Jack's roller case, and I stuffed mine in the backseats, after I had folded them down. The 911 wasn't the most spacious vehicle in the world, but it had other qualities. A convertible wasn't available, so we were making do with a sunroof. That was fine by me. In weather like this, I didn't want to drive with the top down. Hell, even with the sunroof closed, the sun blazed through the tinted glass.

I glanced at the side view mirror again. "Can't outrun the radio," I muttered in a matter-of-fact voice.

Jack's eyes flicked to the rearview. "I don't see him."

JD jammed the brakes, and the car stopped on a dime. He turned onto FM 4212 and punched it again. The road twisted through the hills, and we were quickly out of sight from the main highway.

The nav screen adjusted and calculated a new route.

This road was a little smaller, a little bumpier. It had a few more twists and turns.

My eyes kept flicking to the mirror. I was pretty sure the sheriff couldn't have seen us turn off. A small county like this didn't have a helicopter. Who knows how many other patrol units they had?

I'm sure there would be one waiting ahead of our original destination.

I soaked up the scenery, watching the lazy cows chewing on grass. We passed a dead armadillo upside down on the shoulder.

The landscape was rugged yet beautiful.

This was hard country.

The sheriff's patrol unit was the only car that we had seen in miles. There wasn't any smog, no traffic jams, no high-rises to clutter the view. Pure, unobstructed wilderness. The kind of wilderness where you could dump a body, and it might never be found.

A carcass of a jackrabbit lay on the road, buzzards picking at the red, mangled flesh. It was an ominous sign. If that sheriff got hold of us, there might be buzzards picking at *our* flesh.

S nakebite, Texas. Population 3046.

Somebody came out and painted the sign every year to reflect the current status of the population. The town took it seriously. Every soul counted around here.

I wasn't ready to say that we had gotten away clean, but I hadn't seen those red and blue lights in a long time. We made a couple of twists and turns down narrow farm-to-market roads, then cut over to SH 429. It was 100 miles of gray asphalt. The main stretch that would take you to Sable Springs or Coyote Crossing. Those were the big towns. You know, the ones with a Walmart. Snakebite was a rest stop in between, about 50 miles from either metropolis—deep in the heart of Mesquite County.

JD pulled to the junction at FM 4212 and SH 429 and paused a moment, glancing in either direction.

Not a car in sight.

Jack turned onto the highway and headed toward town.

This was the nerve-racking part.

I felt safer on the back roads. Travel SH 429 long enough, and you'd likely run into a sheriff or a Texas Highway Patrol. I had no doubt our escapades had been squawked all over the radio. I wouldn't be surprised if deputies from nearby counties were headed our way to join in the action. It was probably the most excitement this town had seen in a while.

Fortunately, we didn't have far to go.

The Saddleback Ranch was a few miles down on the left.

JD pulled to the white gate that bubbled with patches of rust here and there. Stone walls flanked the entrance, and a steel archway overhead displayed the name with pride. A silhouette of a cowboy riding a bucking bronco was the focal point.

"You want to get the gate?" JD said. "The combination's 5412."

I hopped out, walked around the front of the Porsche, and fiddled with the padlock. An iron chain snaked around the gate, securing it to the post. I dialed the combination into the brass sequential padlock and yanked it loose. The chain rattled and clanked against the gate like rustic chimes. The rusty hinges squeaked and squealed as I pushed the gate open and held it, making sure it didn't drift closed. That would do wonders for the Porsche's paint.

The tires rumbled as JD drove across the cattle guard onto the russet-colored dirt. This car wasn't exactly suited for off-road. The clearance was pretty damn low. Once he pulled through far enough, I closed the gate, locked it, then hustled back to the car and climbed in.

The wondrous countryside unfurled before us—rolling plains, thick scrub brush, and mesquite trees. Giant hay bales dotted the sweeping pastures, and fields of oats and clover glowed a vibrant green. It was a harsh contrast to the thorny underbrush and prickly cacti that covered the landscape. Cows grazed in fields, chewing on grass, mounds of dung piled far and wide. They looked on with curiosity as we rolled toward the main ranch house, dirt and gravel crunching under the low-profile tires.

The sprawling stone estate presided over the countryside. This was no quaint home in the country. It was a virtual castle from which the duke of the land had once ruled his fiefdom. Accented with wood columns and a metal roof that could withstand the harsh Texas elements, this was a house that spit in the face of driving winds, brutal hail, and blistering sun. The grounds around the house were well maintained. The Stars and Stripes and the Lone Star waved from a flagpole in front of the house. There was no mistaking what country you were in—the Republic of Texas.

A three-tier fountain was the focal point of the cobblestone drive in front of the house. Several vehicles were parked out front—the requisite four-wheel-drive pickup truck, jacked up and covered in mud, scratched from plowing through heavy brush, a heavy-duty dual-cab diesel for hauling cattle trailers, a Mercedes SUV, and a sporty white Mercedes SLK convertible. Those were just the cars that were visible. I'm sure there were some gems in the six-car garage.

Large oak trees provided shade around the house. But even the shade didn't offer much respite from the blistering sun.

JD parked the car, and we hopped out. By the time we climbed the steps to the portico, Tiffany McAllister was there to greet us.

This wasn't the kind of place you could pull up to unannounced. Someone would see you coming. If you didn't belong, you'd risk getting shot.

Tiffany's face was tormented with a mix of joy and sadness. She rushed to greet JD with a hug and held on tight.

"I'm so sorry," he said, offering his condolences.

Tiffany's eyes misted, and she sniffled.

She was a gorgeous young blonde, still in college at the University of Texas. Normally, she'd be in the dorm this time of year, but an unfortunate event called her home.

She broke from the embrace, sniffled, and said, "Thanks for coming."

Tiffany looked at me with those sad blue eyes and gave me a hug as well.

"The last time I saw you, you were knee-high to a grasshopper."

"Well, I've grown up a little since then."

"A little," I said in an understated tone.

She had certainly blossomed into a stunning young woman.

Her father, Jim McAllister, had been in the Teams. When he got out of the Navy, he moved back to Texas. He'd come into a little bit of money and had reacquired most of his family's land that had been lost after his father made some bad financial moves.

JD had served with Jim longer than I did, and he kept in touch with him over the years.

"Come on in," Tiffany said. "Get out of this heat. Can you believe it?"

"Yes, I can, actually," JD said.

"It's never *this* hot this time of year."

She escorted us into the home.

It felt like a lodge.

There was a large vaulted foyer with stairs that led to the second floor. Jim's office was off the foyer to the right. To the left was a large parlor with leather furniture, a minibar, and a flatscreen TV.

Beyond the foyer, a central hallway was the main artery that fed the two wings of the house. To the left, the kitchen, the laundry room, a guest bathroom, and finally, the sprawling master bedroom. To the right, a rec room, a bar, a weight room, and the garage.

We crossed the hall and stepped into the living room. The high vaulted ceiling was planked with wood. Rustic columns became places for decorative knick knacks—rusted horseshoes, Texas stars, and old spurs. Comfy brown leather sofas and chairs decorated the area, along with busts of trophy animals that hung on the walls—regal 14-point bucks, antelope, and elk from Jim's adventures in Colorado. Large windows offered a view of the pool, the rolling hills beyond, and the majestic Coyote Canyon Lake to the north. In a place like this, it would be easy to believe you were the only person in the world. There wasn't a neighbor as far as the eye could see—683 acres of solitude.

"Can I get you anything to drink?" Tiffany asked.

"Probably too early for whiskey," JD said.

I looked at him, astonished. JD wasn't normally one to pass on a drink, no matter what the time. But this wasn't an ordinary case. This was Jim McAllister. A buddy. A friend. A brother in the Teams.

"Tell us what's going on," Jack said.

3

"This whole thing has been a nightmare, and it just keeps getting worse," Tiffany said, her eyes misting again. Her throat tightened, and she broke down into sobs.

JD put a comforting arm around her. "It's going to be okay. We're going to get to the bottom of this."

She sniffled and brushed the tears away. "They found him at Widow's Point. It's on the northwest corner of the ranch. He'd been shot." She could barely get the words out.

"What was he doing out there?" JD asked.

She shrugged. "I'm sure he was hunting. He had his .25-06. He loved that gun for deer."

"Who found him?" I asked.

"Cole," she said. "He's the ranch hand. Dad hired him a couple years ago. He helps with the cattle, fills feeders, sows oats, mows the grass. You name it."

"Does he live on the property?"

Tiffany nodded. "In the guesthouse." She motioned to the northwest side of the mansion.

I glanced across the pool and saw the freestanding structure just off the west wing.

Tiffany continued. "The sheriff hasn't done shit."

"These investigations can seem like they're going nowhere, but it takes time to put everything together," JD assured. "Especially in a place like this."

Time moved as slow as molasses in this part of the country.

"It's unacceptable. At first, the coroner said it was a homicide, then came back and said it was an accident. Said a stray bullet must have come across from the neighbor's property. I don't buy it for a second."

"Did Jim have a problem with the neighbor?" I asked.

Tiffany gave us a look like the term *problem* didn't even begin to describe it. "They did NOT get along."

"What was the issue?" I asked.

"Well, Earl is just an asshole in general, but when my dad bought the property back from the Cavanaughs, there was a dispute between him and Earl about the fence line. According to the survey, it had been mis-marked for years, and my dad wanted to re-fence that border accurately. Earl didn't want to hear anything of it. It wasn't that big of a deal, really. We're talking 15, 20 yards difference. Things got a little complicated a few weeks ago. Earl shot a deer on our property. Said he shot it on his side, and it jumped the fence. Dad pitched a fit, and they got into it. Words were exchanged."

She sighed. "I don't know. That's what I got secondhand. I wasn't here."

"We'll have a word with Earl," I said.

"Dad's body wasn't found far from the fence line."

"Is Cole on the property now?"

Tiffany nodded. "Yeah. He's out on the front 40 working on the fence." She frowned. "You guys have to help me. I haven't even told you half of it yet."

We both listened with curiosity.

Tiffany hesitated. "Let me just check on something."

She hustled to the hallway and called to the master bedroom, "Blair?"

There was no response.

Tiffany stepped into the foyer, peered out a window, then returned. In a hushed tone, she said, "As if my father's dying wasn't bad enough, Blair shows up with a new will that leaves the property and my dad's entire estate to her. It was signed last week. She had it notarized and everything."

"I take it that's a change from his previous will?"

Tiffany nodded. "Dad revised his will shortly after they got married. He gave me a copy of it. He was very clear about the property staying in the family. He had set aside a generous amount for Blair, but the will stipulated that she could only stay in the house in the event of his death until the time that she remarried. He wasn't keen on letting it go to someone else. Now I'm cut out completely. Of course, Blair said I can stay here until I graduate." Anger flushed her cheeks. "They'd been married for less than a year. Now she has everything."

"You suspect the new will is fake?" I said.

"I'm sure it is." She exhaled and admitted, "But Blair has a way of clouding a man's judgment." Her voice was thick with disdain. "Hell, she's only a few years older than I am."

"How did they meet?" I asked.

Tiffany scoffed. "Do you really want to know?"

4

Blair burst through the front door, making a grand entrance, her high heels clattering against the tile as she strutted into the living room. She lowered her oversized Chanel sunglasses and looked at us with curiosity.

Blair was a striking woman. No doubt about it.

Her platinum blonde hair, big blue eyes, full lips, and hour-glass figure were the stuff of fantasy. She wore a white wide-brimmed hat and a form-fitting dress to match. It was past Labor Day, but nobody was going to complain to Blair about wearing white this time of the year. With a figure like that, she could wear anything she wanted or nothing at all. Men would drool, and women would glare with envy.

"I didn't know we were having guests," she said in a slightly snooty tone.

"Blair, this is Tyson and JD," Tiff said. "They're old Navy buddies of my dad's."

Blair extended her hand in an elegant, southern manner. Her nails gleamed with a perfect French manicure, and her skin was smooth and creamy.

JD took it with grace. "Pleasure to meet you."

"Charmed," I said.

Blair smirked.

She oozed sexuality.

The vixen could elevate pulses the moment she walked into a room. It was easy to see how a man could lose his better judgment around her. I'm sure those ruby-red lips could whisper things in your ear that would make you defy logic and reason. She had the most delightful southern drawl. Her diamond earrings sparkled, and so did the rock on her finger. It was half the size of Texas.

"They came for the funeral," Tiffany continued. "I told them they could stay here."

Blair did her best to hide her irritation. She flashed a smile. "Any friend of Jim's is a friend of mine. Feel free to stay as long as you like. Make yourselves at home. Mi casa es tu casa."

Tiffany maintained a smile as she tried not to throw up in her mouth. "They're deputies in Florida. I thought they might be able to help with the case since Sheriff Donnelly isn't doing anything."

Tiffany hadn't come out and said it yet, but I knew she suspected Blair of having some hand in her father's demise. I'm not sure why she told Blair we were deputies other than to watch her squirm.

Blair hesitated a moment and did a double take. "You two don't look like deputies."

JD smiled and said his favorite phrase, "We are a special crimes unit."

"Well, my husband certainly was special. He meant the world to me. So anything you can do to assist is more than welcome."

"Thank you. Jim was a good friend."

"I'm sorry we had to meet under these circumstances. I didn't get to know a lot of Jim's friends." She paused. "You say you're old Navy buddies."

"Yes, ma'am," JD replied.

"Jim still talked about those days often. I think he secretly missed them."

"Tiffany was just giving us some of the details, telling us about the problems with Earl."

Blair rolled her eyes at the mention of his name. "I wouldn't be surprised if he set up across the fence line and waited for my husband. This was no accident. Jim certainly didn't shoot himself with his own gun. That's what they tried to say at first, but the story keeps changing."

"I hate to be graphic, but do you know if the medical examiner was able to recover a slug from the body?"

Both ladies shivered.

"I don't know," Blair said. "That's a little out of my area. I don't think to ask those kinds of questions."

"Hopefully, the local lab can run ballistics," I said.

"I wouldn't count on the local lab for much of anything," Tiffany said.

"Were you here the day it happened?" I asked Blair.

She frowned and nodded. "Jim went out in the afternoon to hunt and check the fence line. He liked Widow's Point." She groaned. "Ugh, that name. I never gave it a second thought before now." She paused. "He said there were a lot of deer that moved through that area in the afternoon, and he had seen a nice size buck back there and wanted to get a better look." She put her hand to her heart. "I, personally, am not a hunter. But I do enjoy a good piece of venison from time to time."

"So, you were here at the house?" I asked.

"Yes. I expected Jim to return in the evening, but he never did." Her eyes misted, and she paused for a dramatic moment to compose herself. "I sent Cole to look for him. That's when..." her throat tightened, and she couldn't go on.

We gave her a moment.

Tiffany regarded her performance with skepticism, but she tried to keep it stifled.

Blair pulled herself together. "Cole called me, and I called 911. The sheriff and EMTs arrived, but there was nothing they could do." She teared up again.

"Is the sheriff pursuing any leads besides Earl?" I asked.

Blair huffed. "I don't think the sheriff is pursuing any leads. In his defense, he's got his hands full right now. With everything that is going on at the border, there are a lot of things happening right now."

"You're not anywhere near the border."

"Doesn't matter. They're using some of these poor people as drug mules, or so I hear," Blair said. "They're carrying back-packs full of cocaine north hundreds of miles. In this heat, no less." She frowned and shook her head. "Hank said they found a body over in Silverton County. Poor girl died of heat exhaustion. They figured the cartel made her carry drugs all the way up here from the border, then left her behind when she couldn't make it. It's tragic. And I think those drugs are making their way into the community. It wasn't long ago when Grayson overdosed."

"Grayson?"

"Star quarterback for the high school."

"Who's Hank?"

"Sheriff Donnelly. He thinks Jim may have run into poachers or the cartel. He says whoever killed him could be long gone by now." Blair frowned again. "I hope that's not true. I mean, I don't want them anywhere around here, but by the same token, I want whoever is responsible brought to justice."

"We'll do our best."

"Do you have any authority here?"

"We're just a tad out of our jurisdiction," JD said. "But if we find something, maybe we can convince local law enforcement to take action."

"And if they don't?"

JD shrugged. "Let's just say that justice will be served."

Blair looked impressed. "Well, thank God for you two."

"Have you had any incidents with trespassers or poachers on this property prior to this?"

"We've heard shots that sounded like they were on the property, but sound carries around here sometimes, depending on the wind," Blair said. "Plenty of trespassers and petty theft. I don't know who's responsible, but if you don't nail it down, it's gone by morning."

Tiffany said, "Somebody broke into the stables and stole some feed, and it looks like someone spent the night in there once. They left a few nice presents behind, if you know what I mean."

"Absolutely disgusting," Blair commented.

"I'd like to talk to Cole when he's available," I said.

"I'll call him and tell him to come to the house," Blair said.

5

"Yeah, I can take you there," Cole said.

He had joined us in the living room after Blair called.

We said our goodbyes to the ladies and followed him out of the house.

"Nice truck," I said as we stepped under the portico.

"Thanks."

He'd parked the Antimatter Blue Metallic Raptor by the fountain. With giant, knobby tires and a supercharged V-8 putting out 700 hp, it was a hell of a work truck.

We climbed into the dual cab, and JD took the backseat. Cole fired up the engine, put it into gear, and headed down a dirt path. The vehicle had considerably more ground clearance than the Porsche and was orders of magnitude more useful around these parts. But I don't think it would outmaneuver the highway patrol.

In his mid-20s, with ice-blue eyes, Cole had rugged good looks, a square jaw lined with a few days of stubble, shaggy dark hair, and the muscles of a farm boy used to carrying 50-pound sacks of feed. His bronze skin was tanned by the intense sun, and he was coated in the requisite amount of dirt and grime for someone who spent his days laboring around a ranch. There was a little grease and dirt under his fingernails that probably never got fully removed. He wore jeans, cowboy boots, a sleeveless T-shirt, and a backward baseball cap.

You couldn't keep a truck like this clean around here. Five minutes after a wash, it was coated with that incessant red dust. The kind of dust that permeates everything, including your nostrils. It lined the exterior and the interior.

Bro-country music filtered from speakers in the cab. It wasn't necessarily my first choice of music, but it had some redeeming qualities. This particular song was about the good country life—friendly girls in cut-off blue jean shorts with their feet on the dash of your pickup truck. The song included references to beer, football, God, country, and the simple life.

Out here, far away from the chaos of the big city, the simple life sounded really appealing. Get a piece of land, a nice house, a good woman, and raise a strong family. Be self-sustaining. Grow your own food, raise your own cattle, collect your own eggs, and tune out from the madness.

But apparently, even a place like this wasn't safe from the madness. Like a weed, it spread far and wide.

We bounced across the terrain as Cole drove us deep into the property. The vast ranch had varied topography. There were dense thickets, wide open plains, rolling hills, high ridges, steep cliffs, a small creek, and plenty of wildlife. An old railroad right-of-way served as the main artery. The tracks had long since been removed, and it snaked through the terrain like a highway. Nestled on the banks of Coyote Canyon Lake, the ranch offered prime access to boating, fishing, and other water sports activities. The reservoir was deep and relatively clear. Popular with scuba divers, swimmers, and boaters, it saw plenty of action on hot summer days.

I was surprised that the area wasn't more developed, but it was in the middle of nowhere. I'm sure it wouldn't be long before developers started putting condos on the lake and turning this sleepy town into a resort destination. But people around here weren't quick to sell their property to developers. Most of the land had been in families for generations. The pace was slow, and people liked it that way.

The truck rumbled as we cruised through the acreage, kicking up dirt and gravel. We turned off the main thoroughfare onto another dirt path that weaved through craggy mesquite trees. We finally reached a stopping point, and Cole killed the engine. We hopped out and made the rest of the journey on foot.

"It's usually not a problem this time of year, but with the heat, keep an eye out for rattlesnakes," Cole said. "They like to sun themselves on the trail."

There were plenty of diamondbacks in the area.

Even in the dead of summer, this wasn't the place to wear shorts. Thorny twigs and jagged branches loved to scratch ankles and shins.

We weren't exactly dressed for the occasion. Jack wore his traditional uniform of a Hawaiian shirt, cargo shorts, and checkered Vans. I was in a T-shirt, shorts, and sneakers. This had me rethinking my choice of wardrobe.

We were a long way from the Florida Keys.

"How did you find the body?" I asked as we followed Cole.

"Jim had told me he planned on hunting Widow's Point in the afternoon. When he didn't return, Blair called me in a panic. There's a blind up here not too far from the fence line. Lots of big bucks come through the trail. It's always been good hunting here, hence the name. Makes a lot of widows out of the doe."

The rough underbrush grabbed us as we marched down the path. We moved through a densely wooded section, then came to a clearing. Fifty yards beyond was the fence line. It was a skewed boundary of twisted barbed wire and faded mesquite fence posts.

I pointed to it. "Is that Earl's property on the other side?"

Cole nodded. "This is right where I found Jim," he said, stopping on the trail at the edge of the tree line. "It was horrible. I'm no expert, but it looked like he was shot with a high-powered rifle. He had his .25-06 with him, and at first, there was some speculation that maybe he shot himself accidentally." Cole shook his head. "But that's ridiculous. Jim knew his way around a weapon."

"That's for sure," JD said.

It hadn't rained since the incident, and the crimson stains still splattered the grass and a nearby tree. It was dark and dry—the color of a Pinot Noir. The splatter told part of the story. It was a clear indication of the direction from which the shot was fired.

6

I pointed at the fence line. "It definitely came from that direction. Probably Earl's property, but it's hard to say."

"That was my thought," Cole replied.

I asked him about the dispute, and he said pretty much the same thing that Blair did.

"Have you had much of a problem with poachers?" I asked.

"I hear shots, but by the time I get to where I think they're coming from, nobody's there. But I've seen a lot of people moving across the property."

"Blair mentioned."

"You wouldn't think you'd have to do it around here, but you gotta lock your doors these days. It ain't what it used to be. I've had shit stolen from my truck. Excuse my language."

"No worries. How long have you been working here?" I wanted to see if it matched what Blair told me.

"Oh, I'd say going on two years now."

"How was your relationship with Jim?"

"Great. Jim was like a father to me. He was an easy guy to work for as long as you did what you were supposed to. If you didn't, he let you know about it. Some people didn't like that, but I didn't mind. The way I see it, you work for a man, you do the job you're paid for, and you do it well. Jim took care of the people who did right by him."

JD nodded in agreement.

"He helped me get that truck," Cole continued. "Co-signed for it and everything."

"That's mighty generous of him."

"He was a good man," Cole said with a frown, his sad eyes falling to the dirt.

"How'd you come to work for Jim?" I asked.

"He had Dusty and Buck doing things around here for a while, but those jackasses couldn't do anything right. He fired them, and I happened to bump into Tiffany in town. She said her dad was looking to hire. I needed a job. The timing was perfect, and it worked out."

"Tell me about Dusty and Buck," I said.

"Couple of idiots. Jim caught them stealing. Doesn't surprise me. They've been in and out of trouble as long as I can remember."

"What kind of trouble?"

"You know, typical stuff—drinking, fighting, disorderly conduct. That kind of thing. They've spent a few days in

Sheriff Donnelly's lockup here and there. Couple of losers, if you ask me."

"I would imagine there was some bad blood between them and Jim."

"I don't think they were on the best of terms. The way I heard it was they still wanted to be paid for the work they had done, and Jim told them to go to hell." He paused. "You think they might have had something to do with this?"

I shrugged.

"That was a couple years ago."

"Sometimes people carry grudges for a long time," JD said.

"That's certainly true around here. There are feuds in this town going back a hundred years. People grow up hating other people, and they don't even know why."

"Who do you hate?" I asked.

Cole raised his hands innocently. "I don't hate anybody. I just go with the flow, do my job, and try to get along."

"Do you get along with Blair?"

"Yeah. Like I said, I try to get along with everybody."

"Did you ever... *get along*?"

He finally caught on. His brow crinkled. "No. That's Mr. McAllister's wife!"

"She's an attractive woman. You're a handsome young man."

"I don't know where you come from, mister, but that kind of thing is frowned upon around here. If you value your life, you don't put your hands on another man's woman."

I couldn't disagree.

"Plus, Jim always kept a loaded shotgun close by."

"Do you know how they met?"

Cole hesitated. "I don't think that's my place to say."

I regarded him with curiosity. I was beginning to have an idea, but I didn't press the issue. "What about you and Tiffany?"

"We dated for a minute before she left for college. Kind of a summer thing, I guess."

"How did that end?"

He shrugged. "She was going off to school, and I was staying here. We knew from the beginning it wasn't going to go anywhere. I don't think Tiffany was looking for a guy like me. I don't think she wanted to get stuck in this town. She wanted to get out of here. Hell, who could blame her? She's going to marry some fancy city boy—a doctor, a lawyer, somebody with a career. Me, I'm just simple. Not too sophisticated. I like my truck, my dog, country music, good food, good friends, and a few beers here and there. I ain't looking for much."

"Some people might say that's all you need," I said.

"Well, I would agree with those people."

He seemed like a good guy. But I wasn't making any judgments about anything just yet.

"Is she seeing anybody now?"

"Not that I know of, but we don't really talk much."

"Does it ever get awkward? You working for Tiffany's dad?"

"Things ended on good terms. We stayed friends. If it would have been awkward, I don't think she would have told me about the job opening."

"Have you guys ever... *rekindled* your romance?"

Cole's brow knitted again. "I don't see how that has anything to do with Mr. McAllister's death."

I shrugged. "Just trying to get a sense of things around here."

"No. We've stayed friends."

"How was Jim's relationship with Blair?"

Cole hesitated. "I don't think it's really my place to say."

7

C ole had my curiosity. I urged him to continue.

"They were pretty much newlyweds."

"That doesn't really answer my question."

"I think they were happy. I mean, who wouldn't be with a woman like that?"

I figured he was trying to be sensitive about private matters, but it was coming off as a little evasive.

"Go ahead and speak your mind," I said.

"Look, I need this job. I don't want to speak out of turn. I guess, technically, Blair is my boss now."

"Technically, the estate is still in probate and will be for a while," I said.

"I don't know much about that kind of stuff."

"Did Jim ever discuss specifics of his will with you? Make his intentions known about his wishes after he was gone?"

Cole shook his head. "We didn't talk about that kind of thing. Jim felt like he was going to live forever. Don't we all?"

There was an awkward pause between us.

"Look, there were some rumors that Jim had reconnected with one of his old high school flames. Brooke Barnes."

"Was there anything to the rumors?"

Cole shrugged. "I don't know. Like I said, I try to keep my head down and out of other people's business. Especially my employer's."

"Was Blair aware of the affair?"

"I don't know if there was an affair. You know how small-town gossip is. Somebody sees you with somebody else, they automatically think things. There may not be any truth to it whatsoever."

"Did you ever see them together?"

"No. But people asked me about it." He paused. "Seems kinda crazy to me. Brooke Barnes is not exactly in the same league as Blair."

"Sometimes it's about more than looks," I said.

"True."

"Is Brooke Barnes married?"

Cole nodded.

I exchanged a glance with JD.

"I wonder, did her husband know about the alleged affair?"

"It was the talk of the town," Cole replied. "I would imagine so."

I surveyed the area, then moved along the trajectory of the bullet to where I estimated the origin might be. I walked all the way to the fence and didn't see any shell casings. I looked over the fence at Earl's property—more mesquite trees, scrub brush, and cacti. There were plenty of places to take cover and get a clear shot at Jim as he exited the wooded path and entered the clearing at Widow's Point. I wasn't particularly inclined to hop the fence and traipse around somebody else's property, especially one who might have a gun. This was Texas. You didn't cross property lines.

I returned to the bloodstains, photographed the area extensively, then Cole escorted us back to the truck.

The sun angled toward the horizon. The Texas sky turned shades of orange and pink, casting long shadows.

We climbed into the truck, and the bro-country blasted. We bounced and bobbled back to the main house. I exchanged numbers with Cole and told him to get in touch if he thought of anything else.

Cole pulled to the front of the house. "I got more work to do, but I'll be around if you need anything."

We thanked him again and hopped out of the truck. He drove away, and we climbed the steps and entered the foyer.

"Tiffany?" JD shouted. "We're back."

She emerged from a bedroom on the second floor and hurried down the hallway. She spiraled down the stairs to greet us in the foyer. "Did you see what you needed to see?"

I nodded.

She shivered. "I just didn't think I could go out there and look."

"I understand."

"Listen, I've got to run back to Austin and grab something from my dorm. Why don't you two get settled into your rooms, then we'll go into town and grab dinner before I head out. How does that sound?"

"That sounds fine by me," JD replied. "When are you coming back?"

"In the morning. Don't worry."

She escorted us upstairs and showed us to our guest rooms in the east wing. The rooms had rustic charm, painted in earth tones. My room was decorated with longhorns, Texas stars, and leather chairs. I had a clear view of the pool, the guest house, the stables, and all the way down to the lake. A 27-foot motor yacht with a slate gray hull and white trim was docked at the pier.

We hustled down to the Porsche, grabbed our bags, and dumped them in the rooms. JD and I rejoined Tiffany in the foyer, and the three of us left the comfort of the AC and stepped back into the heat.

"Just follow me into town," Tiffany said as she hopped into her SLK. "And don't speed around here. Sheriff Donnelly is a hard-ass about that stuff."

JD grinned. "Never."

I climbed in with Jack, and we followed her across the property. We rambled down the dirt road to the main gate. She hopped out and thumbed through the sequential combination, unhooked the chain, and pulled open the gate.

I climbed out and held it for the cars, then locked up and hopped back in with JD.

Jack turned onto the highway and cruised behind the SLK to the Sagebrush Steakhouse. We parked next to Tiffany and hopped out.

"Smells good," I said.

"The best in town," Tiffany replied with a smile.

I grabbed the door for her, and we stepped inside. The hostess recognized her right away and looked at us with curious eyes. "Table for three?"

Tiffany nodded.

Gossip would spread quickly in this town. *Who were we? What was she doing with us?*

The hostess grabbed three menus and escorted us to our table. The restaurant had a good crowd. The air was filled with the delightful scent of grilled meat and tangy seasoning. It had more of that Texas charm. Fancy, but unmistakably rural at the same time.

We took a seat and perused the menu.

"Order whatever you like. It's on me," Tiffany said.

"You don't have to buy us dinner?" JD replied.

"I want to. It's the least I can do. It was so good of you both to drop everything and come when I called."

"No trouble at all, really," JD assured.

The menu was full of typical offerings—bone-in ribeye, filet mignon, tomahawks, sirloin, and an array of sides. Garlic mashed potatoes, sautéed spinach, sautéed mushrooms, French fries, curly sweet potato fries, vegetable medleys. There was a surf and turf option, but we weren't anywhere near the ocean, so I stuck with the eight-ounce filet, sweet potato fries, a side of mushrooms, and I'd settle on dessert later.

A delightful waitress with a southern accent attended to our table with a smile. We ordered a round of drinks to start off, and Tiffany stuck with diet soda. She told us about her college experience. It was good for Tiffany to focus on something besides her father for a moment. A little break from the sorrow.

"Scarlett's doing well," she said to Jack. "I'm such a fan."

Jack beamed with pride. His daughter had firmly established herself in Hollywood as a bona fide star.

"I'm so excited for her. Does she just love it?"

"I think she's having the time of her life."

"Seems so glamorous," Tiffany said with a dreamy look in her eyes. "When I was a kid, all I could think about was escaping this town and moving to the big city. Now all I want to do is come back and continue the legacy that my father was building."

"Priorities change," Jack said.

"Yeah, but that wretched woman is going to take that legacy and squander it. I bet she sells the place before my dad's body is in the ground."

"Do you think there is something going on between her and Cole?" I asked.

Her face twisted with revulsion. "I'd like to think that Cole has better taste than that, but sometimes men do stupid things."

"Yes, we do," JD said.

"You guys have two brains, and we all know which one is in charge," she snarked.

A couple passed by the table and recognized Tiffany. The woman was in her 40s with auburn hair. She said, "I'm so sorry about Jim. If there's anything we can do, please don't hesitate to ask. We're here for you."

Tiffany flashed a grim smile, took the woman's hand, and thanked her. She introduced us to Mr. and Mrs. Lawson.

"Pleasure to meet you both," Valerie said. "What brings you to town?"

"They're old friends of my dad's," Tiffany said.

I think Mrs. Lawson was more curious about us than she was about offering condolences to Tiffany.

"Well, I'm so glad you could be here for Tiffany."

"So are we," I replied.

We made small talk for a moment before they left.

The waitress returned with our entrées not long after. My filet was tender and juicy. Grilled to perfection, wrapped in bacon, and slathered with garlic butter and lemon pepper. I had no complaints. This place knew how to cook steak, as well they should. We were in the heart of cattle country.

After we ate, the waitress came by with a dessert platter that had a sample of everything they offered. Key lime pie, cheesecake, chocolate mousse, German chocolate cake, fresh berries with whipped cream. It was all sinful.

"You have to get the strawberry cheesecake," Tiffany said. "It is divine."

"Strawberry cheesecake it is," I said to the waitress.

She returned with three Texas-size wedges that would put you into a sugar coma. Creamy and tangy with a graham cracker crust and a few slices of fresh strawberries, drizzled with red strawberry sauce. I'd had a lot of good desserts in my day, but this made my taste buds happy.

JD tried to pick up the tab, but Tiffany wouldn't let him. She paid the bill, and we thanked her for dinner.

"So, what kind of trouble are you looking to get into tonight?" Tiffany asked.

"I figured we'd kick around town, ask questions, get a feel for the local flavor," JD said.

"Well, you've got a couple of options. There's the Rattlesnake Saloon, the Cactus Club, and the Honky-Tonk Palace, but I don't think that's really your speed. If you want to go down to the lake, there is the Buzzard's Roost. And if you two are looking for a little company, you can go to the Pleasure Pony or the Silver Saddle. Just be careful—you might come home with a wife, or a disease, or both. Kinda like dad did." She said in an unamused tone. "Not the disease. The wife." Then she thought about it. "Maybe she is a disease."

"So that's where he met Blair?" I said.

"Yep. My stepmother is a stripper."

"Was," JD clarified. "Now she owns a ranch."

Tiffany scowled at him. "Ugh. Don't remind me. You have to do something about that. I mean, come on. My father dies, and she magically turns up with a new will that gives her everything?" She rolled her eyes dismissively. "Please."

"We'll talk to the notary that witnessed the document," I said.

Tiffany paid the tab, and the three of us strolled out of the restaurant, fat and happy. But that's when the real bill came due.

We said our goodbyes for the evening. Tiffany gave us both a hug, and JD and I ambled to the Porsche.

Two sheriff's cars screeched into the lot and blocked us in.

Black and white hot-rodded Dodges with sleek graphics. The sheriff's logo and star emblazoned in gold on the door panels. It was the same type of vehicle we had encountered on the highway.

It was time to pay the piper.

Officers emerged with guns drawn. Angry pistols stared us down.

8

"On the ground! Now!" the sheriff shouted.

He wasn't playing around.

Tiffany looked on with wide eyes as JD and I ate the pavement.

"What's going on?" Tiffany asked.

The sheriff and his deputy pounced. Soon, my arms were wrenched behind my back, and handcuffs slapped around my wrists, right on the bone. It didn't feel so great.

"We're cops," I grunted.

The concrete was still hot from the afternoon sun. I was glad this didn't happen at midday.

"I don't give a good goddamn who you are."

They frisked us, found our weapons, and eventually our badges.

JD got the better end of the deal. The woman who pounced on him was cute. If I had to get arrested by anybody, I'd choose her. Golden blonde hair pulled into a tight ponytail, blue eyes, and a petite little figure. A woman in uniform that knew how to use a gun... she was checking all the right boxes. If I wasn't on the wrong side of this, I'd think she was really nice. She sure made the uniform look good. Her gold name plate read: *Deputy Sawyer*.

"What's going on?" Tiffany asked again.

"Stay out of this, Tiff," the sheriff snapped. "It ain't none of your concern."

"They're with me, Sheriff!"

I couldn't see his face, but he paused for a moment.

"Coconut County," he said, surveying my badge. "You boys are a long way from home."

"They're friends of my dad's," Tiffany declared. "They came here because I asked them."

"I guess speed limits aren't a thing where you come from," the sheriff said.

"I'm not sure what you mean," I replied innocently.

"You two know damn good and well what I mean. Did you not see me pull out behind you? I guess you were traveling too damn fast at 162 miles an hour."

He looked at JD. "And you are the son-of-a-bitch that was driving."

This was the point where we probably should have kept our mouths shut. But like most idiots, we tried to talk our way out of it.

"We were in hot pursuit," JD said.

"Chasing a suspect all the way from Florida?" the sheriff groaned.

"Yes, sir."

"A smart-ass, huh? Where's that suspect now?"

"He got away."

"Either of you dipshits know what happens when a deer jumps into the road in front of you at that speed? Besides ruining that fancy car of yours, you both get antlers up your ass."

"That doesn't sound fun," Jack said.

"No, it doesn't. And you know who has to scrape your guts off the asphalt when it's all over?"

"I figure the buzzards will take care of that."

"I ought to take you two out there and leave you for the buzzards."

I got the impression he may have done that before.

The sheriff clenched his jaw and exhaled a frustrated breath. "You know how many laws you broke? Speeding, reckless driving, reckless endangerment... I'm thinking about making up some shit. I ain't never clocked somebody coming down that highway at 162 miles an hour. What the hell do you think this is? The goddamn Indy 500?"

JD wised up a little. *A little*. "I'm sorry, Sheriff. I take full responsibility. Poor judgment on my part. The road looked wide open, and the scenery so beautiful, I just lost myself in the moment."

"Well, you're gonna lose yourself in the county lockup. It will be for more than a moment, too."

"You're right. I absolutely deserve it."

"Sheriff, they're here for the funeral," Tiffany said. "They were in the Navy with my dad. Can you let them off with some kind of warning?"

Donnelly grumbled for a moment. He exchanged a glance with Deputy Sawyer.

She gave a slight shrug.

After a long, tense moment, Donnelly said, "If I ever catch you two idiots doing that kind of speed on my highway, I promise you, as God is my witness, you will never get out of my jail."

"We will obey all posted road signs," I assured.

"I want to hear it from this dipshit," he said, pointing at Jack.

"You've got my word, Sheriff."

He nodded to the blonde, and they both unlocked the cuffs. They stood up, and we pushed off the ground.

Donnelly handed back my badge and weapon. "The only reason that you two are walking away from this right now is because of this young lady." He motioned to Tiffany. "Jim McAllister was a good man, and if you two idiots served with him, you can't be half bad."

"Thank you, sir," I said. "You have our deepest gratitude."

He huffed slightly, seeing straight through my ass-kissing. "I expect you two will stay out of trouble for the rest of your stay in my county."

"Absolutely, sir."

"And may I remind you... you two may be law enforcement, but you ain't here."

"We're just visiting," I said.

"That badge is not a get-out-of-jail-free card."

He stared me down for a long moment.

Hank Donnelly was a hard man. Dark hair, peppered with gray, narrow brown eyes, a square jaw with a dimpled chin, and lines on his face that were a roadmap of the years. He wore a cream straw cowboy hat, a khaki duty shirt with brown epaulets rimmed with gold piping, and brown pants to match. The gold Texas Star pinned to his chest read Mesquite County, his name etched in gold on the plate above.

After a moment, he nodded to his deputy, and the two strolled back to their patrol cars. She had a nice strut.

They climbed into the cars, pulled the doors shut, flicked off the swirling lights, and rambled out of the parking lot.

The adrenaline began to wear off, and my heartbeat slowed. I breathed a sigh of relief.

"What the hell did you two do?" Tiffany asked.

"We may have failed to pull over," JD said.

"162 miles an hour?"

"Give or take," JD said. "We still had plenty of room to run. That was just when he clocked us. We got way faster after that."

Tiffany's eyes rounded. "You're lucky the sheriff didn't shoot you on sight. He just loves to write tickets to out-of-towners. He'll take you down for 20 miles over. It's a big source of revenue for the county."

"I bet," I said.

"I'm afraid to leave you two alone for the evening."

"We'll be on our best behavior," JD assured with a wry smile.

Tiffany was smart. She didn't buy it for a second.

"When are you coming back? You don't want to miss the funeral tomorrow."

"I won't miss it. I'll turn around and come back early in the morning. Maybe even tonight."

"That's a lot of driving in one evening."

She smiled. "I do it all the time. Plus, the drive is soothing. I need something to occupy my mind right now."

"Be careful," JD cautioned.

"I will."

We said our goodbyes, and she climbed into the SLK. JD and I hopped into the Porsche and decided to recon the local watering holes.

9

The Rattlesnake Saloon looked like as good a place as any to find trouble. The red neon sign out front glowed, and a coiling viper wagged its tail. Something told me it was easy to get bitten in a place like this.

It was a 51% establishment, and there was a posted sign. According to Texas law, concealed firearms were prohibited in establishments that derived 51% or more of their sales from alcohol. The federal LEOSA act permitted qualified and retired officers to carry in all 50 states, but it didn't supersede private property rights and didn't exempt officers from certain federal locations and "gun-free safe zones." Most bad guys managed to overlook the nuances of the law. We'd already been in enough trouble for the day, and we weren't on official business, so we decided to leave our pistols under the seat for good measure.

I felt a little naked, walking into the bar without one.

The sound of pool balls clattered as we entered, and Southern rock blared through the speakers. It was a typical roadhouse bar with Texas flags draped on the walls, along with old license plates, arrowheads, horseshoes, road memorabilia, and rusted railway spikes. There was a dartboard, a central bar, a dance floor, a small stage for the occasional live band, and several booths and tables. Neon beer signs glowed behind the bar.

We moseyed up to the counter and took a seat.

The bartender gave us a curious look as she approached. She was mid-40s and a little leathery with stringy blonde hair. Skinny as a rail. Something told me she spent all her free time at the lake, soaking up the Texas sun. "What's your poison?"

"Whiskey. Rocks," JD said.

"Make it two," I added.

"Paying cash, or do you want to start a tab?"

"I'll pay cash."

Everybody liked cash customers.

The bartender grabbed a bottle of whiskey, spun it around like a gunslinger, and filled our glasses. Ice crackled and popped. She slid the drinks across the counter and told JD the charge. He slapped a wad of cash on the counter. "Keep the change."

"Much obliged."

He left a generous tip. The drinks were less than half the price of comparable whiskey in Coconut Key. We might have to drink twice as much.

"I ain't seen you, fellas, around. New in town?"

Jack smiled. "Just visiting."

She squinted and gave him a side-eye. "Not too many people visit Snakebite, Texas."

"What's not to love?" JD asked with a grin. "Wide-open spaces. A nice lake. A friendly town."

She chuckled. "You ain't been here very long."

"Just got in town today, and the sheriff gave us a warm welcome."

She gave him a look, knowing better. "Now I know you're full of shit. I only suspected it before."

JD laughed.

"What really brings you to town?"

JD smiled. "I'll never tell."

"I gotta do my due diligence. Everybody's gonna ask questions. People know they can come to me for answers."

"What's your name?" JD asked.

"Billie, but you can call me BB, Babe, Sugar, Honey, or Darlin'."

"Well, aren't you sweet, Darlin'," JD said, mirroring her accent.

She smiled, and her blue eyes sparkled.

"I'm Jack Donovan, and this is my buddy Tyson Wild."

"Pleasure to meet you," she said, extending her hand. There was nothing dainty about it. This was a woman who worked for a living. "Now that we know each other, what are you really doing here?"

"You're persistent, aren't you?"

BB smiled. "I usually get what I want."

"I have no doubt."

JD told her we were friends of Jim's, and she offered her condolences.

"He was a really nice guy," Billie said. "Not like some of these other rich assholes."

"Good people," JD said.

"So, Billie, since you know everything in town, what do you think happened?" I asked.

She gave me a look and considered the question for a moment. "Any number of things. But I can tell you right now, for a fact, that Jim McAllister didn't shoot himself. If I had to wager a guess, I'd say he stumbled across somebody poaching on his property or trespassers. You never know who's out there in the wilderness these days."

"That seems to be what the sheriff thinks, though I really haven't spoken to him about it."

"Well, I don't think they're ever going to find out who did it."

"Why do you say that?"

"It's been a couple days, and I ain't heard talk of a suspect. And you know what they say... the first 48 are the most important. The longer it goes unsolved, the more likely it will remain that way. And it's not like we've got a crack squad of investigators around here. The biggest crime

Donnelly deals with around here is some guy beating up his old lady, somebody stealing cattle or horses, drunk drivers, and speeders on the highway. He was in here earlier today asking around. You should have seen him bitching up a storm about those two assholes tearing up the highway. Clocked them at 162 miles an hour. That was the talk of the town. I wouldn't be surprised if it makes the headlines tomorrow. What kind of moron do you have to be to drive that fast?"

"I hope he caught those guys," JD said, trying to keep a straight face.

"Let me tell you, if Sheriff Donnelly caught them two, we might be having three funerals in this town."

JD and I exchanged a subtle glance.

"You know Earl Jackson?" I asked.

"Honey, I know everybody in this town."

"There's talk..."

"I've heard the talk." Billie shrugged. "I don't want to go pointing fingers at the man. He can be grumpy and cantankerous. But that describes half the population here."

"Why is that?"

"There's always something to bitch about."

I laughed.

"You can either complain, or you can be grateful," JD said with a smile. "I choose gratitude."

"You must be rich to think that way."

Jack laughed.

"Don't get me wrong," Billie said. "I thank the good Lord each and every day for another one. As tough as it is, it still beats the alternative."

"Nobody said it would be easy."

"Amen."

We sipped the fine amber liquid and surveyed the establishment. It wasn't crowded by any stretch of the imagination. A couple guys occupied pool tables, and a delicious blonde flitted about. She wore a tight cut off tank top tied at the waist, exposing her midriff. Blue jean shorts, like the country-western boys sing about, gave everyone something to drool over. Her smooth, toned legs planted themselves in rattlesnake cowboy boots. She had the eye of just about every guy in the bar.

"Don't get any funny ideas," Billie said, noticing our distraction.

"Why is that?" JD asked.

"She's nothing but trouble."

JD smiled. "Oh, but I like trouble."

Billie chuckled with amusement. "Somehow, that doesn't surprise me. You two had trouble written all over your faces the moment you walked in here."

We feigned innocence.

"Don't give me that. You two are little devils. I can tell." Her eyes narrowed as she sized up both of us. "Good at heart, though."

We smiled.

"Amen," JD said, lifting his glass.

We clinked and sipped the fine whiskey.

Billie had seen a lot of people come and go. She was quick to get someone's number.

Being new to town, we stuck out like a sore thumb. We had drawn plenty of curious stares when we first stepped into the saloon. It didn't take long for the little blonde vixen to stagger toward the bar and post up beside us. She leaned on the counter, squeezing her endowments together, forming a delightful valley of cleavage. She knew she had magnetic qualities. She pretended to ignore us for a moment. "Billie Ray, I'm empty. Fill me up."

Billie Ray took her glass, refreshed the ice, and mixed another cocktail. "Whose tab am I putting this one on?"

She looked at JD and batted her long eyelashes. "You wanna buy me a drink, Daddy?"

The words rolled off her slick tongue with a breathy, innocent naughtiness that elevated pulses.

She was trouble indeed.

10

A sucker is born every minute.

JD said, "Put it on my tab."

"You don't have a tab," BB replied.

Jack dug into his pocket and slapped a few bills on the counter.

"Thank you, Darlin'," the blonde vixen said in an adorable drawl. She stared deep into JD's eyes. "You ain't from around here, are you?"

"We're new in town."

"Just passing through? Or are you staying for a while?"

"I don't know. That depends."

"On?"

"If I got a reason to stick around."

She smiled. "I can think of plenty of reasons."

"I bet you can," JD said, enthralled.

Her eyes squinted at him. "You look familiar."

"I just have one of those faces."

"You ain't like a serial killer, are you?"

JD laughed.

"You wouldn't hurt little old me, would you?"

"I'm harmless," JD said with a smile.

She extended her hand. "I'm Nikki."

JD made introductions.

BB watched with amusement.

A couple of guys at a pool table took notice of the interaction. They didn't look too pleased about it. I had a sense they'd be trouble before long.

A young redhead stepped into the bar with a stack of flyers in her hand. She looked a little too young to be in this place, and Billy Ray didn't hesitate to shout at her. "Nope. You can't be in here."

"Take a pill, BB. I'm just passing these out," she said, displaying the flyers."

"I let you put one of those up on the door, and I let you pass some out yesterday. You can't be in here every day. If the sheriff catches you here, I'm gonna be the one in trouble."

"Fuck him. He ain't gonna do shit."

"Watch your language, Maddie."

"You ain't my mother."

"You should be nice to me if you want to pass those out in here."

"I'm being nice. I just saw new cars in the parking lot and thought there might be new people." Maddie looked at us and handed JD and me each a flyer.

On the page was a black-and-white photo of an adorable young girl with soft features. She looked about 14 or 15. In bold font across the top of the page, the flyer read: MISS-ING. Below the picture was a description of the girl and her last known whereabouts. There were pull tabs with a phone number to call.

"You ain't seen my sister, have you?" she asked us.

"No. Sorry," I said.

According to the date on the flyer, Gracie Hutchins had been missing a couple of weeks.

"Tell me what she was doing the night she disappeared," I said.

"She was babysitting for the Lockwoods. They say she left the house at about midnight. She'd have to ride her bike this way to get home."

"Where's home?"

"Just up the road a bit, then take a right on Hickory Hollow, and a left on Lafayette, then go down about 2 miles, and it's on the right."

"So she had to ride home along the highway?"

"Did it all the time."

I exchanged a look with Jack. Any number of things could have happened.

"Anybody ever find her bike?" I asked.

Maddie shook her head, and her blonde hair swayed. She had beautiful green eyes and a light dusting of freckles on her cheeks.

"How old are you?"

"17. Gracie was just about to turn 15."

"My sister's name is Madison," I said.

"Everybody calls me Maddie."

"I assume the sheriff is looking into this."

"Yeah, but he ain't done shit. He thinks she ran away. She wouldn't run away without telling me."

"Got good reason to," BB said.

"What reason would that be?"

Maddie and Billie exchanged a glance.

"That's a long story," Billie said.

"She didn't run away," Maddie insisted. "She didn't take any of her things. Didn't pack a bag. Some sicko's got her. Probably got her locked in a dungeon somewhere."

"It's possible that somebody picked her up on the highway," I said.

Sadness tormented Maddie's face. "Gracie could be halfway across the country now. Sex trafficked. She could be dead in a ditch." Maddie broke down into tears.

My heart broke for the girl.

"Has the sheriff contacted the FBI?"

"I don't know what he's done. I mean, he came out to the trailer and talked to Wade. Talked to the people she was babysitting for. I've been to every bar and restaurant off the highway, asking if anybody saw anything the night she disappeared."

Tears flowed.

"Does your sister have a boyfriend?"

"She was talking to Zeke. But they ain't official or nothing."

"Is this your number on the flyer?"

Maddie nodded. "That's my cell."

"We're going to be in town for a few days. I'm not gonna make any promises, but we'll look into it."

"I appreciate that, mister. Are you some kinda cop?"

I gave a discrete flash of the badge, and Maddie's face brightened with hope.

"That would mean so much to me. Please, you gotta find her," she said, clasping her hands together in prayer.

"I'm gonna be upfront with you. These cases are tough. Gracie's been gone for almost two weeks now. Hundreds of people come through this highway every day."

She frowned. "I know."

"Did she have any troubles with anyone?"

"Well, Wade. But everybody's got trouble with him."

"Who is Wade?"

"Mom's boyfriend. I can't wait until I get my own place. I don't know what Mom sees in that loser."

I was starting to get a picture of the situation. I could only imagine the full details.

"What's your sister's cell phone number?" I asked.

"Believe me, I've tried calling it. She doesn't answer."

"I may be able to track the phone."

"Really?"

"Maybe."

She gave me the digits, and I gave her my card and told her to get in touch if she thought of any additional details.

"Thank you, mister. I really appreciate this."

She moved on and passed out flyers to everyone in the bar.

I texted Isabella Gracie's number and asked her to pull the phone's GPS history.

Isabella was in charge of one of the most powerful clandestine agencies. They were an *off-the-books* kind of place with virtually unlimited intelligence resources. They were the kind of organization that gave other agencies plausible deniability. Her means of acquiring intel wasn't always legal, and we couldn't use what she gave us in a court of law, but it often made things a lot easier.

"I didn't figure you two for cops," Billie said.

Jack smiled and said his favorite phrase.

"Oooh! Special Crimes," Nikki said. "That sounds exciting."

"Gracie is such a sweet girl," BB added. "I hope you find her. But she wouldn't be the first girl to go missing off the highway."

"That's scary," Nikki said. "You never know who's out there. Any one of those people passing by could be a sicko."

Nikki finished her drink, then jiggled her glass. A few thin pieces of ice rattled. "Looks like I'm empty again." She batted those eyelashes at JD. "You gonna fill me up, Daddy?"

JD was powerless. "Give the lady what she wants, Billie Ray."

BB refreshed her glass and mixed another cocktail.

"Now, you wouldn't be taking advantage of me, would you?" JD asked.

Nikki flung her arms around JD's neck and stared deep into his eyes. "I would never take advantage of you, Sugar. Not unless you wanted me to." Her naughty voice danced across his ears, and her eyes smoldered.

JD was entranced.

The guys at the pool table had seen enough. The two marched in our direction with scowls on their faces.

11

"What the hell are you doing, Nikki?" the dirtball asked.

His brown, greasy hair hung to his shoulders, and his puffy, narrow blue eyes were glassy and bloodshot. A scraggly goatee sprouted on his chin. He was about 6'1" and wiry. The lean kind of muscle that comes not from the gym but from ranch work.

His buddy was a little shorter with slicked-back dark hair, smarmy eyes, and a weaselly nature to him.

"Having a drink, meeting new people," Nikki said.

"You're acting like a fucking whore is what you're doing," the dirtbag replied.

Nikki's face twisted. "Shut up, Dusty! I'll act however I want to act." She returned her attention to JD and smiled. "You don't think I'm acting like a whore, do you?"

Dusty fumed.

I put two and two together that this was Dusty and Buck.

Jack stood up and got in Dusty's face. "I think you need to apologize to the lady and move on."

Dusty scowled at him. "Who the fuck are you?"

"The guy who's gonna put a foot in your ass if you don't beat it."

I was off the bar stool by this time and ready for anything.

The muscles in Dusty's jaw flexed, and his hands balled into fists.

I flashed my badge to diffuse the situation before it got out of hand. "I think your bar privileges have been revoked for the evening. Beat it!"

Dusty squinted at the badge. "You ain't got no authority here."

Nikki stuck her tongue out at him.

Buck shifted on his feet, his eyes flicking between the two of us. He glanced at Dusty for his cue.

"I don't think this is something you want to follow through with," I said. "It won't end well for either of you."

Dusty scoffed. "You talk tough, big man. But you'll go down like all the rest. Why don't you put that badge away and take this outside?"

"Walk away," I said.

"Run along, Dusty, before you get your ass kicked," Nikki taunted.

He glared at her, then his eyes flicked back to JD and me. He contemplated the situation.

Dusty was smarter than he looked. "Fine. You want to act like a whore, act like a whore." He raised his hands in surrender. "Makes no never mind to me. I wash my hands of it."

He thumped Buck on the arm and nodded toward the door.

We watched them go, then returned to our barstools.

"Sorry about that," Nikki said. "He means well. He just gets a little overprotective sometimes."

"Who is that?"

"My brother."

"I'm sorry," JD said.

"Tell me about it. I had to grow up with that."

"They used to work for Jim McAllister, right?" I said.

Her face wrinkled with confusion. "How did you know that?"

"We were friends with Jim."

"They worked for him a long time."

"It's my understanding there was bad blood."

"As you can see, it's not hard to get crossways with Dusty," Nikki said. "You boys just got into town and already got the makings of a feud that could last a lifetime."

"He doesn't seem to respect authority," I said.

"Dusty doesn't respect much of anything."

Something told me Dusty and Buck wouldn't be quick to answer questions about Jim McAllister.

Maddie made the rounds and stopped by to thank us again before she left.

We ended up staying at the saloon until it closed. I kept a cautious eye on the door in case our friends returned. Nikki flirted with Jack and told us all about the town. JD bought a few rounds for everyone in the bar just to get on good terms with some of the locals. You never know when a friend might come in handy, especially in a place like this.

"I just want to assure you that I am not a whore," Nikki said to Jack. "But I do need a ride home. Unless, of course, you want me to walk, and we all know what can happen to a sweet young thing walking alongside the highway at night."

"I believe we can accommodate that request," JD said.

"I mean, I think I can trust you. You're both cops."

"You're in good hands," JD assured.

"I have no doubt," she said with a sparkly smile.

We thanked BB, then left the Rattlesnake Saloon and stepped out into the muggy night air. Jack dug the key from his pocket and slapped it into my palm. He'd been going drink for drink with Nikki, and that girl could handle her liquor. I'd been pacing myself. Besides, I think he had worked out the logistics in his mind and chose the most favorable option.

JD escorted Nikki to the Porsche.

"Son-of-a-bitch!" he groaned when he got close.

12

Someone had taken a key to the car and carved a trench in the GT Metallic Silver paint. The canyon ran the length of the car.

It didn't take a rocket scientist to figure out who did it.

"That son-of-a-bitch is asking for trouble," JD muttered.

"Gotta prove he did it," I said, walking around to the driver's side. I didn't have the heart to tell Jack that this side was gouged as well.

"I'm sorry," Nikki said, cringing.

"It's not your fault."

"It sort of is."

"Nonsense. You're a grown woman. You can make your own choices."

She smiled. "That I am."

He pulled open the door, climbed in, and offered her a seat on his lap, which she readily obliged. She slid in and cozied her rear up to his crotch, putting a wide smile on Jack's face.

For a moment, JD forgot all about the enhancements to the paint.

"At least it's a rental," I said as I climbed behind the wheel.

"Yeah, but they're going to charge me for the damage."

"Could be worse," I said.

I fired up the engine, and the exhaust growled.

"This is a fancy car," Nikki said. Then she realized, "It was you two that gave Sheriff Donnelly trouble on the highway."

Jack smiled. "Guilty as charged."

Nikki laughed. "I would love to have seen his face when you blew by him on the highway."

I backed out of the space, rolled out of the lot, and turned on the highway. I was mindful to keep it under the speed limit. "Where are we headed?"

"You're gonna travel down SH 429 for a few miles, then take a right on Sawdust. I'll tell you from there."

I had just turned onto the highway when a patrol car appeared behind me. I looked in the rearview, waiting for the red and blues to spin up. I glanced down at the speedometer and was still under the limit. I couldn't tell who was in the patrol car, but I had no doubt the sheriff spread the word to all his deputies to keep an eye on us.

We turned off the highway onto Sawdust, and the squad car kept rolling down 429. Nikki gave me directions, and we bounded down the back roads. After a few twists and turns, we ended up on a narrow dirt road, kicking up dust. Gravel crunched under the tires and bounced around the wheel wells for a while, then we turned onto a small piece of property and stopped at the gate. Nikki hopped out, got the gate, and I drove through.

She closed it, hustled back around, and resumed her throne. I drove her up to a small one-story brick house.

"You live here alone?" JD asked.

"Nope. Me and Dusty. And Buck is almost always here, so it's like I've got two roommates. But I don't see Dusty's truck."

"Lucky for him."

"It was our folks' place until they passed. Dusty and I have been living here since."

I pulled up to the house and put it in park.

"Thanks for the ride, gentlemen."

She opened the door and hopped out.

JD followed. "I'll escort you to the door."

I watched from the car as he walked her to the porch. She gave him a hug and a kiss on the cheek, then slipped inside.

He started back to the Porsche with a grin on his face.

"I have half a mind to wait around for that dirtball and give him a piece of my mind," Jack said when he climbed back into the car. He pulled the door shut and buckled his seatbelt.

"Let it go. Not worth it."

I spun the car around, and we headed back toward the gate. Jack hopped out, stumbled toward it, and pulled it open.

He rejoined me after I drove through, and we headed back toward Saddleback Ranch.

"You remember how to get to Jim's?"

13

Tiffany had given me a key. She hadn't returned yet. The SLK wasn't in the driveway.

We tried to make as little noise as possible as we slipped in through the front door. JD staggered up the stairs to pass out in his guest room. I was a little hungry. I figured I'd sneak into the kitchen and see what I could rustle up for midnight rations.

I tiptoed through the darkened house into the luxurious kitchen filled with state-of-the-art appliances. There was a nice gas range with a grill that was perfect for cooking up steaks if the outdoor grill was unavailable due to inclement weather.

I pulled open the stainless steel refrigerator, and the glow from the interior light illuminated my face as I perused the items. I found some roast beef, sliced cheese, and mayonnaise. Along with the wheat bread on the counter, it would make the perfect midnight sandwich.

I turned around to set the items on the butcher block and caught a glimpse of Blair. She stood in the doorway holding a pistol, wearing a white sheer négligée with nothing on underneath. In that instant, I knew exactly what Jim McAllister was thinking when he married her.

She wasn't shy or bashful at all. I don't think she minded me looking through the négligée for an instant or two or three.

The pistol in her hand was concerning.

"Sorry, I forgot we had company. I heard a noise in the kitchen, and well... You can't be too careful these days."

"True."

She set the pistol on the butcher block.

"You don't mind if I fix myself something to eat, do you?"

"Go right ahead. But while you're at it, I'll take a little snack too."

I lifted the package of roast beef and asked if it was acceptable.

"Perfect."

She guided me to the plates, and I whipped up two sandwiches.

"How have you been enjoying our town so far?" she asked.

"It's been interesting." I told her about our introduction to the sheriff and our meeting with Dusty and Buck.

"By the end of tomorrow, I'm sure you will have met everyone in town."

"Almost," I said with a smile.

I don't think she was really hungry. She took a few bites of her sandwich, and that was it.

We stared at each other for a long, awkward moment. The pale moonlight filtered in through the windows, and she drew a little closer. "I'm really glad to have someone here. It's terribly lonely now that Jim is gone."

"Well, you've got Tiffany to keep you company."

"It's just not the same." She looked at me with those seductive eyes.

The invitation was subtle, but it was there. Most men would jump at the opportunity. I don't think Blair was used to having to drop more than a subtle hint.

Maybe she was lonely, or maybe she was just trying to see how good of friends I was with Jim.

"What are your plans for the ranch now?" I asked.

"I haven't really had time to think about it. The last few days have been a whirlwind, trying to make arrangements, dealing with grief, consoling Tiffany. It's a terrible tragedy." She took a breath, then sighed. "I'm sure I will continue Jim's legacy. It's what he would have wanted." She paused. "Who knows, he always did say that I was bigger than this town." Blair bit her bottom lip as she thought. "They say you shouldn't make big decisions in a time of grief. Give yourself a year. I think that's what I'll do. I'll give it time and reassess."

"I think that's a wise plan."

She took another seductive nibble of the sandwich, those blue eyes working their magic.

There was another long, awkward silence.

I didn't take the bait, as enticing as it was.

"Well, I should get back to bed. I'm just down the hall in the west wing if you need anything."

That invitation wasn't subtle.

"Thank you. I appreciate your hospitality."

"No trouble at all."

She spun around and sauntered out of the kitchen, the négligée flowing, her pert assets jiggling.

I took a breath, starting to sweat.

My phone buzzed with a call from Isabella. It wasn't good news.

14

"What are you doing in Texas?" Isabella asked.

I told her.

She offered her condolences. "You're picking up a couple cases while you're there?"

"Might as well, and Maddie seemed desperate."

"You're a kind soul, Tyson."

"I can't turn my back on people."

"That's what I like about you. But I don't think you're gonna like what I'm going to tell you."

I cringed.

"Gracie's phone was on Highway 429 around 12:30 AM the night she disappeared. Looks like she had ridden her bike all the way from the Lockwood residence, then gotten a flat, judging by the velocity of travel. She was probably walking the bike along when she got picked up on the highway. Her phone moves at 65 miles an hour and is driven down to the lake, then goes off the grid. Cell service is pretty spotty in that area. Coverage isn't great. Notwithstanding, it doesn't bode well for your missing person."

My jaw tightened.

"You want my honest opinion?"

"I know what you're going to say. You think she's probably at the bottom of that lake."

"Somebody picked her up, something happened, and they dumped the body."

"Makes sense."

"You might want to convince local law enforcement to send a dive team out."

I laughed. "I don't think we're going to convince local law enforcement to do anything."

I told her the situation.

She laughed. "Making friends."

"Always."

I ended the call and ambled up to my guest room. As I was crawling into bed, I heard a car pull into the driveway. The front door opened moments later. I figured Tiffany had returned.

I woke with the morning sun as amber rays spilled through the blinds. The delightful aroma of bacon and coffee swirled. I pulled myself out of bed, showered, dressed, and made my way down to the kitchen.

Tiffany grilled at the stove. She had prepared a feast. Bacon, eggs, hash browns, sausage, pancakes, waffles.

"Smells good."

"Help yourself."

I poured myself a cup of coffee and dished up a plate of pancakes and a couple slices of bacon. I smothered the stack with butter and maple syrup and took a seat at the kitchen table. "You got in late."

"Yeah, I decided to make a quick turnaround. I slept for a few hours but got up early and decided to busy myself with breakfast. I have so much anxiety right now."

"Understandable," I said. "Try to let it all go. The stress doesn't help anything."

"I know."

JD staggered into the kitchen a few moments later. He took in the spread with impressed eyes. "Well, look at this!"

Tiffany smiled. "We like breakfast around here. Plus, cooking soothes my nerves."

They both dished up a plate and joined me at the table.

Blair stepped into the kitchen a moment later. "Good morning, everyone." Her eyes found Tiffany. "I see you made it back safely. I heard you come in right after the boys last night."

Tiffany forced a smile.

There was a little tension there. Maybe a lot.

It was probably a good thing Tiffany didn't walk in on us in the kitchen last night. It might have looked a little funny.

Blair dished up a plate and joined us at the table. "Thank you for the sandwich last night," she said to me. "It hit the spot."

That drew a curious stare from Tiffany.

I got the impression that Blair liked to stir up trouble.

After breakfast, we got dressed for the funeral. I wore a Donatello Conti suit, a Bertolucci tie, and shoes by Mario Moretti.

Jack looked respectable for a change. His suit was, dare I say, normal. An abrupt departure from his usual, over-the-top nature. But this was a somber time, and his outfit was appropriate. He pulled his hair into a slicked back ponytail and wore dark aviator sunglasses. He looked like a cross between a Mafia hitman and a rock star.

Blair, as always, was impeccably dressed in a tight strapless black dress, elbow-length black gloves, and a wide-brimmed black hat with a veil. Her makeup was done to perfection. You'd think she was attending fashion week. A diamond choker sparkled around her elegant collarbones. Dark sunglasses covered her eyes.

She looked like a movie star or royalty.

Tiffany was dressed in an understated, elegant black dress. Unlike Blair, she didn't look like a character from a '50s noir. Blair was every bit the femme fatale, and she played the part well.

Cole drove Blair and Tiffany, and we followed in the Porsche to the Holy Star Cathedral. Flowers adorned the entry hall. Tiffany and Blair greeted guests as the procession filed into the church and took their seats.

An older gentleman with shaggy gray hair, bushy brown eyebrows, and an oversized mustache approached Tiffany. He had a narrow face that was lined and looked like saddle leather. He was tall and skinny and had spent a lifetime working a ranch in the Texas sun. His weathered hands took Tiffany's, and he expressed his condolences. His voice was deep, and his jaw tight. "I'm deeply sorry for your loss. If there's anything I can do, please don't hesitate to get in touch."

Tiffany thanked him, and he moved on to offer his condolences to Blair.

She whispered, "That's Earl Jackson."

I was surprised he showed up after hearing about the feud. I planned on talking to him after the service.

Sheriff Donnelly arrived with the pretty blonde deputy. Donnelly gave us a stern look as he approached. "I hope you two are staying out of trouble."

"Yes, sir."

He didn't buy it for an instant. He moved on and offered his condolences to Tiffany and Blair.

The blonde followed behind him.

"Deputy Sawyer, so good to see you again," I said.

She just looked at me and said nothing as the procession continued to move through.

After the family had greeted all the guests, there was a brief mass, followed by the interment at Serenity Valley.

The heatwave persisted, and the priest kept his words brief.

The Ceremonial Guard played taps and handed Blair a folded flag on behalf of a grateful nation. She wailed and cried, making a show of it.

Tiffany stifled her reaction.

I noticed a woman had arrived that wasn't at mass. She kept her distance from the family, and I suspected it might be Brooke Barnes. I asked Tiffany, and she confirmed my suspicion. I hadn't talked to her about the alleged affair yet and figured now wasn't exactly the time.

Brooke was in her late 50s with strawberry hair, a round face, and pretty blue eyes. I think she was a little heavier than she'd have liked, but she was probably quite stunning at 21. Still cute, but certainly not Blair McAllister.

Once Jim's coffin was lowered into the ground, she'd seen enough and started for her car. I discreetly caught up with her. "Excuse me, are you Brooke Barnes?"

Her face wrinkled with confusion. "Yes. Who are you?"

I flashed a subtle glimpse of my badge. "I'm Deputy Wild. I just have a few questions for you."

I didn't bother to tell her I was with Coconut County. People often see the badge and leave it at that.

In a hushed tone, I said, "I know this is a difficult time, and this is a difficult question, but can you tell me the nature of your relationship with Jim McAllister?"

She looked a little flustered. "We were... longtime friends. We went to high school together."

"I heard you were high school sweethearts."

"Yes. So?"

"Did that relationship rekindle?"

"Absolutely not," she said, her brow tight. "Jim was a married man. I'm a married woman."

"Those facts do not preclude attraction. The heart wants what the heart wants."

"I'm not exactly sure what you're getting at. Whatever it is, now is not the time nor the place."

"Did your husband know about your relationship with Jim?"

"I had no *relationship* with Jim. I told you we were just friends."

"Did you care about him?"

"I cared about him deeply."

"Then you'll start telling me the truth. Somebody killed Jim McAllister, and I'd like to find out who. He was a good friend."

Brooke hesitated a moment, then glanced back to the crowd that was beginning to dissipate now that the ceremony was over.

"I don't know where you've been getting your information, deputy. But you're mistaken. Now, if you'll excuse me..." She turned and walked away.

Sheriff Donnelly noticed our interaction and glared at me.

I made my way back to the crowd and rejoined JD and Tiffany.

Jack muttered, "Did you find anything out?"

"There's definitely something there. She's not talking."

"I think we need to have a word with Mr. Barnes. Maybe he got a little jealous and took matters into his own hands."

Afterward, there was a small reception at the VFW Hall. There were snacks and refreshments. People mixed and mingled, telling stories about Jim. His picture sat atop a table by the guest book.

I found Earl and asked him a few questions.

15

"You need to get that notion out of your head," Earl said. "I wasn't anywhere near the fence line that day. And I know we had our issues, but quite frankly, I'm offended at the suggestion that I might have some involvement in Jim's death. Hell, you think I'd show up at the funeral of a man I shot?"

I shrugged. "Maybe that's just for appearances."

Earl's eyes narrowed at me. "Son, I don't know who the hell you are or what business it is of yours. But I'm telling you right here and right now, as God is my witness, I did not shoot Jim McAllister. If you know what's best for you, you'll keep your distance."

"So you don't have an alibi for that afternoon," I said as he started away.

He turned back. "I don't have an alibi because I live by myself."

He marched away, and the heated tone of his voice carried across the hall. Sheriff Donnelly had taken notice. He excused himself from his conversation and made his way toward me.

I knew this wasn't going to be pleasant.

"What exactly do you think you're doing?"

"Just asking questions," I said in an innocent voice.

"It ain't your job to ask questions."

"I'm just curious by nature."

His jaw tightened, and his eyes narrowed. "I thought you two were just visiting."

"We are. But I can't help but try to piece things together."

"How about you leave that up to me?"

I smiled. "Oh, absolutely. I don't want to step on anybody's toes."

"I can assure you, I've talked to Earl, and I've ruled him out as a suspect."

"On what basis?"

"On the basis that I've known the man for 50-some-odd years, and despite the fact that he can be cantankerous and ornery, he's not a killer."

"But you don't know that for certain."

His cheeks reddened, and he looked like he was about to explode. He took a breath and held back for a moment. In a calm voice that was thick with anger, he said, "I know, because I know."

"Did you search his property? Take a look at his weapons?"

"No, I have not. I don't believe there is probable cause."

"What about ballistics? Have you determined what caliber weapon Jim was shot with?"

"I don't have that information yet. You may not have noticed, but the sprawling metropolis of Snakebite doesn't exactly have its own crime lab. We have to send out for that kind of thing."

"I'd really like to speak with the medical examiner," I said.

"I don't give a good goddamn what you'd like."

"I'm just saying I'd feel better. And I know Tiffany would feel better if we had all the information."

"She will get all the information in due time as soon as it becomes available. I can't produce answers out of thin air. But rest assured, I, and my entire department, are doing our due diligence to bring the perpetrator to justice. Now, you know as well as I do that in a situation like this, there are no easy answers. This could be a transient. The perp could be miles away from here by now. We might never find out what really happened."

"Kinda like Gracie Hutchins' disappearance. She could be anywhere by now."

Hank's jaw tightened again. "I see you're taking on missing persons cases now."

"It's kind of a hobby of mine."

His cheeks reddened again, growing tired of my snarky remarks.

"You might want to send a dive team out to the lake and look for her."

"Now, why in the hell would she be at the bottom of Coyote Canyon Lake?"

"I think somebody picked her up from the highway, did bad things, killed her, and dumped the body."

"You figured all of that out in a day?"

"That's what her cell phone records indicate."

His brow knitted with confusion. "Now, how the hell do you have her cell phone records? We've contacted the service provider, and even I don't have that information yet."

"Let's just say that I have sources."

"What kind of sources? Oh, that's right. Excuse me, you're from the big city."

"Coconut Key isn't really a big city. It's more of a small island, actually."

He was about to blow his lid again. "Gracie Hutchins had every reason to run away. She always talked about going off to Hollywood to be a star. And that dirtball stepfather of hers would be enough to drive anybody away. I can't say for a fact, but I think he was probably abusing those kids."

"So he just gets a pass?"

Donnelly scowled at me. "He doesn't get a pass. I don't know how it works in Coconut County, but here, we need evidence of a crime. Neither one of those girls would go on record, and he denied everything when asked. I can't do much when the witness is uncooperative. I'm sure they're afraid he'd beat the living daylights out of them. It's a tragic situation, and it breaks my heart, but I can only do so much. Their mother's a meth head, and those girls have no place to go."

"Why not bring in Child Protective Services?"

"Child Protective Services has been out to the trailer a few times. They've asked questions, evaluated the situation, and found no grounds for removal. Haley managed to clean up her act for a time. And even if they did find grounds for removal, they'd put those girls in a foster home, and around here, they might end up in a worse situation." He paused. "Now, I'm sure you two are fine deputies. But you're in my county now. Let me handle my business. Enjoy your stay, keep your nose out of trouble, and we'll get along. Keep going like you're going, and we won't. Let me tell you, my bad side is not a place you want to be. And you boys are inching really, really close."

A look of surprise flashed on my face. "You mean we're not already on your bad side?"

He clenched his jaw, and a slow exhale flowed from his flared nostrils. "You're trying my patience, boy."

Tiffany saw the drama and intervened. "Sheriff, thanks so much for coming. It means a lot."

16

S heriff Donnelly took a moment to steady himself, then put on a gentler face. "You know I'm here if you need anything."

"I appreciate that, Sheriff," Tiffany said.

By this time, Deputy Sawyer had joined the party.

"If you'll excuse me, I best be on my way." Donnelly gave the deputy a nod, and the two officers ambled out of the hall after he gave me another scowl.

"You're going to have to be a little more discreet about your investigation," Tiffany whispered.

"Yeah, sorry."

"It's not going to do me any good if he runs you out of town."

The reception wound down, and we packed up the leftovers and headed back to the ranch. Tiffany was exhausted and emotionally drained. Plus, she'd been on the road for most of the night and had little sleep. She went up to her room and took a nap.

"I have got to get out of this dress," Blair announced. "Wearing black in this heat will be the death of me."

She sauntered to her room, and we changed out of our suits and into casual clothing. By the time we returned to the living room, Blair was in a skimpy white bikini. The suit clung to her pert form, and the fabric hugged her smooth skin. With a beach towel draped over her shoulder, she strutted across the living room toward the patio. "You boys feel free to take a dip. It's the only way to cool off."

She bounced onto the patio, spread her towel on a lounge chair, then dove into the crystal water.

We were transfixed.

Blair swam across the pool and back, then climbed the steps, dripping wet. She looked like a goddess, her wet hair slicked back, water beading on her skin, the white fabric turning somewhat translucent, leaving nothing to the imagination.

"I really hope she didn't kill him," JD said, taking in the scenery.

"Why do you say that?"

"'Cause Jim didn't stand a chance. That girl could feed you poison, and you'd ask for more."

Blair reclined on the lounge and dripped dry.

We weren't going to get to the bottom of this thing sitting around here. I wanted to speak with the notary, Audrey Davis, and see if everything was above board with the will.

I called Isabella and had her run background. She told me some interesting things.

udrey Davis lived in a little country home on Peach Blossom Lane. It was a quaint one-story on two acres of land. A few live oaks and cedar trees dotted the property, and the field was full of wildflowers that gave it splashes of color. The house was old, and paint peeled from the siding in places.

Audrey answered the door after a few knocks with a crying toddler on her hip in diapers. She was late 20s, early 30s, with auburn hair, tawny eyes, and a narrow face. She had a slim figure and wore a floral sundress.

I flashed my badge and made introductions.

Her nervous eyes flicked between the two of us. "Is there some kind of problem?"

"We just have a few questions for you," I said. "I hope we're not interrupting anything."

"No, not at all." Her face wrinkled with confusion. "Are you new to the department? I thought I knew all of Sheriff Donnelly's boys."

"We're conducting a separate investigation."

"Oh, I see. I suppose this is about Jim McAllister?"

"In a roundabout way, yes."

"Please, come in."

She stepped aside and led us down the foyer into the living room and offered us a seat at the kitchen table. Another small child played with monster trucks in the living room, making engine noises while the TV played cartoons.

"Can I get you anything to drink? Water, tea, coffee?"

"No, thank you," I said.

The house was simple but cozy. There was nothing sleek or modern about it. It had likely been built in the 40s and hadn't been renovated.

"You notarized an updated will for Jim," I said, getting down to business.

She tensed a little. "Yes. Just a few weeks ago. I guess it's lucky he made the changes when he did."

"Were you aware of the changes that were made?"

"No, I just witnessed the signatures."

"Is that your full-time job?"

"It's just something I do on the side to make a little extra money. I work at the bank during the week."

"And where exactly was the will notarized? Did they come to the house?"

"They did."

"Both Jim and Blair?"

She hesitated a moment. "Yes, of course."

"What about the witnesses?" I asked. "It's my understanding that self-proving wills in Texas need two witnesses, and all signatures must be in the presence of a notary."

"Yes, that is correct," Audrey said, growing tense.

"And who would those witnesses be?"

"If I recall, Savannah Bloom and Penny Whitaker. I have it noted in my book."

"Do you have contact information for them?"

"I do not."

I had my doubts that Savannah and Penny even existed. "Can you describe them?"

"Young. Early 20s. Savannah is a redhead. At least she was last I saw her. Penny is a straw-colored blonde."

"Who first approached you about notarizing the will?"

"I believe I got a call from Blair."

"Phone records indicate that she called you on several occasions during that time frame, then you contacted her shortly after Jim's death."

She looked surprised and a little worried. "You looked into my phone records?" she asked with a knitted brow.

"Standard procedure, ma'am," I said.

"I called her as soon as I heard the news to offer my condolences."

"Then you called her again just yesterday," I said.

"Just following up to check on her. Poor thing. I can't imagine what she's going through. Newlywed and losing her husband like that."

"I take it you're close with Blair."

"It's a small town. You get to know people. I'd like to think that I'm close with everyone."

"But not close enough to go to the funeral," I said.

"I couldn't find a sitter."

"Just to clarify once again, Jim and Blair came to this house and signed the will in your presence, along with Savannah and Penny."

"Yes, of course. I wouldn't have notarized it otherwise."

"Are you sure it wasn't just Blair, and you did her a favor?"

She looked appalled. "No. That would be illegal and unethical."

"Maybe she paid you a considerable amount of money. There was a rather large cash deposit to your bank recently."

Her eyes rounded.

"The updated will leaves Blair everything and cuts Jim's daughter out completely."

"Like I said, I wasn't aware of the contents of the will. As for the cash deposit, I recently sold a classic car."

"You have a bill of sale handy?"

"I don't. It was a handshake deal." Her unsettled eyes flicked between the two of us. "Gentlemen, I have an appointment I need to get to. I think that's about all the time I have for questions today."

There was an uncomfortable moment between us.

"Do you know where we can find Savannah and Penny?"

"I don't."

"Are they local?"

"Yes."

"I'm sure we'll have more questions later as we continue to look into this. Fraud is a serious crime. I don't know what the penalties are off the top of my head in this state, but I'm sure they're steep."

Audrey swallowed hard.

"If you decide to change your story, get in touch."

"There's nothing to change about my story, and I don't appreciate the insinuation. Now, I'd like you to leave."

We escorted ourselves out and returned to the Porsche. We climbed in, and JD fired up the engine. He spun the car around, drove off the property, and turned onto Peach Blossom, heading back toward the main highway.

"I'm pretty well convinced she's in on it," JD said. "I don't think she had anything to do with Jim's murder, per se, but she padded her pockets with the will."

Knowing it, and proving it, were two different things.

We'd rattled Audrey's cage pretty good. I wanted to track down Savannah and Penny. I figured if we kept up the pressure, someone might eventually crack. I had my doubts as to whether Sheriff Donnelly would listen to us at this point. None of the information Isabella had given us would be admissible. We'd need to get a warrant, and we weren't in a position to get one.

Isabella had also given me phone records for Brooke Barnes. There were plenty of calls and texts between her and Jim at all hours of the night. It went beyond a casual friendship. I didn't have the content of the text messages, but there was something between them. That was certain. I figured Brooke's husband, Cooter Barnes, might not be too pleased about that. He was high on my suspect list as well.

Cooter and Brooke lived on a ranch northwest of Earl's place that boarded Earl's property. I theorized that Cooter could have hopped Earl's fence, traipsed across the property, and set up by the fence line at Widow's Point. It wouldn't be the first time a jealous husband had taken out a romantic rival.

18

W e stopped by Cooter's ranch, but the gate was locked, and we couldn't get on the property. I wasn't terribly inclined to jump the fence and walk up to the main house. There was a bold *No Trespassing* sign on the gate. Red letters against black. *Trespassers will be shot on site.* I figured Cooter was a man who liked his privacy. Most did around here. You didn't get a lot of door-to-door salesmen. *No solicitations.*

We'd have to catch Cooter in town or sit around and wait. It didn't look like anyone was home. There were no vehicles at the house. But he could have been out on the property.

We left and headed into town and grabbed something to eat. Buckaroo Burger sounded like a reasonable choice. There were a lot of restaurants to check out, and we were eager to get a sampling of everything. Buckaroo was an old-school diner with a checkered floor, red vinyl booths, and lots of chrome accents. The marquee touted it as *The Best Burger in the West.* It had a funky sign with cartoonish lettering.

A MISSING flier with Gracie's picture was taped to the door. I hadn't called Maddie yet. I was waiting until we had something more tangible. I didn't want to tell her my suspicions. It was all just speculation at this point. No need to upset her.

A pretty blonde hostess greeted us as we entered and escorted us to a booth by the window.

Country music filtered from the jukebox.

There was a long bar with stools fixed to the floor. You could get milkshakes, ice cream sundaes, fountain drinks, you name it. They offered every imaginable type of burger—quarter pounders, half pounders, and if you had the stomach for it, the full-pound Big Tex Burger. You could get them slathered with cheese, mushrooms, onions, lettuce, tomatoes, mayonnaise, mustard, special sauce, barbecue sauce, whatever you wanted.

Patties sizzled on the grill in the kitchen, and the aroma of grilled beef wafted through the air.

I went with the Lone Star Cheeseburger with mushrooms and a side of Texas Twisters—crispy golden fries with a blend of signature Texas spices. Jack went with the Double Barrel Buckaroo Burger, which was two patties, two slices of cheese, crispy bacon, and tangy Buckaroo sauce on a lightly toasted sesame seed bun.

Janice delivered the meal with a smile, and we chowed down.

The burgers were fat and juicy, full of flavor. I was inclined to agree with the marquee—these were pretty damn good.

After we ate, we returned to Jim's ranch. Cole was at the stables. I didn't see Blair.

We stepped inside and found Tiffany in her room.

"Are you making any headway?" she asked in a hushed tone, not wanting our conversation to be overheard.

"We have some leads to run down. Do you know Savannah Bloom and Penny Whitaker?"

"The two witnesses on the will."

I nodded.

"Friends of Blair's."

"Know where we can find them?"

"Not around here. I haven't seen them in a while. They used to work at the Prancing Pony. But I heard they moved to Austin. Someone else said they had gotten into porn. Wouldn't surprise me."

"And they just happened to turn up to witness the will," I said, thick with doubt.

"See why I don't buy it?"

I frowned. "How you holding up?"

She shrugged. "I'm still here."

"I know it's tough. Just keep your chin up. Jim would want you to stay strong."

"I know." She paused. "What are your plans for the evening?"

"I figure we'll run back into town and see what we can stir up."

"I think I'm going to sit this one out. I don't feel like doing much of anything."

"I don't blame you. You know where Cooter Barnes hangs out?"

"If he's not at his ranch, he's probably at the Tumbleweed Tavern. That's where a lot of the old-timers hang out."

"You'll fit right in," I teased JD.

He sneered at me.

"I think they're having a fish fry tomorrow," Tiffany said. "Cooter's not gonna miss that."

In a hushed voice, I asked, "Do you have a copy of the wills handy?"

"I do." She hopped off the bed and moved to the dresser. She pulled out both the old and the new.

I examined the documents carefully. There were only a few months between the two. I noted the law firm that drafted the new will, then took a look at the signatures.

It was difficult to say. Signatures can evolve over time. Jim's looked similar to me. I was no expert at handwriting analysis, but I looked for telltale signs. The way the "T" was crossed, whether or not the cursive "A" was completed or left unconnected. Jim's signature wasn't exactly legible in the first place.

The witnesses' signatures were barely legible.

I snapped pictures of the signature pages from both wills and forwarded them to Isabella to see what she could come up with. I asked her to track down the two witnesses.

"You think that's your dad's signature?" I asked Tiffany.

"It can't be. He would never cut me out completely. I just don't believe it," she said in a whisper, her eyes filling again.

"The wills were drafted by two different law firms," I said.

"That's the thing. Monty had been handling Dad's legal stuff for years. Why would he go to a new firm? He revised the will after my mom died and named me as executor and beneficiary. Then revised it again after he married Blair. That's this copy," she said, displaying it.

"Maybe Monty retired."

"He's still in business."

"We'll talk to both of them," I assured.

Tiffany nodded.

"You know if there's any life insurance?"

"I don't really know. Dad kept all his papers in the safe in his office, but it's empty."

"Where's Blair?" I asked.

"I haven't seen her in a while."

"Don't worry. We'll figure this out."

She looked at me with hopeful eyes.

"I don't know about you, but after that burger, I'm ready for a nap," JD said.

It wasn't a bad idea. We adjourned to our respective guest rooms, and I crashed out for a minute or two.

In the evening, we headed into town and grabbed some barbecue brisket from The Smoking Longhorn. Mesquite smoked to perfection and pull-apart tender. Drizzled in a tangy homemade sauce and accompanied by sides of beans and slaw, it was the perfect Texas meal served on butcher paper.

The place was simple, with a concrete floor, picnic tables for seating, and Texas memorabilia hanging on the walls. They had pecan smoked chicken halves, cabrito, chopped beef sandwiches, hickory smoked ribs glazed with barbecue sauce, and pulled pork sandwiches.

There were plenty of pickles, onions, and white bread to go along with the meal.

We smelled like barbecue when we walked out of that place. I could certainly get used to this good Texas grub.

We decided to head up to the Rattlesnake Saloon to see what we could stir up. I think JD might have been hoping to bump into Nikki again. I'm pretty sure he'd like to do a lot of bumping with her.

We stepped into the saloon and took the same seats at the bar. We were quickly becoming regulars.

BB greeted us with a smile and had our drinks poured by the time our butts hit the barstools. "Back for more, are you?"

JD smiled. "We just can't keep away."

"You'd get out of this town, if you had any sense."

"It's got its charm. Plus, we've gotten to meet wonderful people like you."

"You're a silver tongue. That's what you are."

JD grinned.

"So, I heard you upset Sheriff Donnelly again."

"Where did you hear that?"

"Word travels fast. I also have it on good authority it was you two that he chased down the highway yesterday."

JD shrugged. "I can neither confirm nor deny."

BB just shook her head. "You two like to live dangerously."

"The world is a dangerous place."

Jack glanced around the bar.

"She's not here yet," BB said, knowing exactly who he was looking for. Billie looked at her watch. "If she doesn't show up in a few minutes, I'll tell you where you can find her."

lmost on cue, Nikki strutted into the bar. She spotted JD and sauntered up next to him with that bubbly smile of hers.

"Well, look who the cat dragged in," JD said.

"We're going to have to stop meeting like this," Nikki replied.

"Oh, I don't think it's a bad way to meet at all," JD said, visibly delighted by her presence.

Billie Ray mixed a drink for Nikki and slid it across the counter.

"Put it on my tab," Nikki said. "Theirs too. I'm buying tonight."

"That's mighty generous of you," JD said.

"Turnabout is fair play. Plus, after last night, I'm embarrassed. I apologize for my brother's behavior. He means well, but he lacks a certain social etiquette. He's not sophisticated like we are," she said, lifting her glass to toast.

"To good social skills," JD said.

The two clinked glasses and sipped their beverages.

BB rolled her eyes.

I asked Billie what she thought about Cooter Barnes.

"Nice fella, why?"

"I hear things."

"What kind of things?"

"Things about Brooke and Jim McAllister."

"I've heard talk, but who really knows?"

"You think Cooter is capable of murder?"

She lifted a curious brow. "That's a pretty bold allegation."

I shrugged. "Just pursuing all possibilities."

"I've known Cooter for a long time. I don't think he's a murderer. Then again, I don't think he'd take too kindly to someone messing with his wife." She thought about it. "He doesn't live far from Jim's place."

"I know," I said in a confident voice.

"I'm not going to speculate. I'll leave that up to you."

"What about Audrey Davis?"

"You don't think she killed Jim, do you?" BB asked, skeptical.

I chuckled. "No. But I'm just wondering if she might be compromised."

I told her about the will and my theory.

"You're just full of ideas, aren't you?"

I shrugged innocently.

"Audrey's recently divorced. I think she's struggling to keep afloat. She's got those two kids, and that deadbeat ex-husband doesn't pay any support."

"Sounds like incentive."

"People do strange things for money," BB acknowledged.

"Do you know Rutherford Van Buren?"

"Ambulance chaser. Why?"

"Would he draft a fraudulent will?"

"I think Ruddy would do just about anything for a buck if he thought he could get away with it. But drafting a will ain't a crime."

"True," I said. "What do you know about Savannah and Penny?"

BB lifted a telling eyebrow. It told me everything I needed to know. "You haven't seen them around, have you?"

"Not in a while."

She told me the same rumors that Tiffany had heard. Nikki chimed in as well and said she'd heard the same thing.

We had a few drinks, and JD enjoyed the evening with Nikki. We played a couple rounds of pool, threw darts, and closed the bar down at 2:00 AM. The evening was uneventful and free of drama until we stepped outside.

Dusty and Buck waited for us in the parking lot. And they weren't alone. They brought three of their closest buddies with them. They glared at us with angry scowls, fists clenched tight.

"Dusty, what the hell are you doing here?" Nikki asked.

"I'm looking for you," JD growled, eager for some payback.

"Looks like you found me," Dusty said with a cocky grin.

"Somebody took a key to my car."

"I wouldn't know nothing about that."

"You wouldn't know about much, would you?"

The statement seemed to confuse Dusty.

He and his gang had clearly been drinking and worked up some liquid courage. With the shiny GT metallic Porsche parked in front of the Rattlesnake Saloon, it wasn't hard to figure out we were here.

"Dusty, why don't you stop embarrassing yourself?" Nikki said.

"You're the damn embarrassment."

"I suggest you boys go home," I said.

"Funny, I was going to suggest the same thing to you. It's time to pack your bags and be on your way."

"You gonna make us?" JD asked, puffing up.

"Dusty, you're gonna get your ass kicked," Nikki quipped.

"Shut up! The only people gonna get their asses kicked are these two."

Neither of us were armed at the moment.

"Let's do this," Dusty growled at JD. "Me and you."

"Just the two of us," he said. "And your buddies. That sounds fair."

Dusty turned to his friends. "What do you think, guys? Want to watch me kick this guy's ass?"

He spun around and tried to sucker punch JD.

Jack saw it coming from a mile away. He ducked, and Dusty's fist rushed over his head. Jack followed with a hard right to Dusty's gut, and he doubled over. Jack came across with a left hook and connected hard with Dusty's jaw. The blow twisted his head to the side, and Dusty stumbled.

Buck and the entourage rushed in, and pretty soon, it was chaos.

Fists flew, and knuckles cracked against flesh.

Nikki screamed from the sidewalk.

Buck charged me.

I sidestepped and used his momentum, helping him slam headfirst into the side of a car. It made a loud clunk that echoed across the parking lot. It took him a moment to regain his wits afterward. Not that he had much to begin with.

We were going to make short work of these guys. I had no doubt about it. But two deputies put a damper on the party. The patrol cars screeched into the parking lot, lights flashing. The deputies hopped out with pistols drawn.

Dusty, Buck, and his crew collected themselves and sprinted away.

The deputies weren't interested in them. They kept their weapons aimed at us and closed in.

One of them shouted, "On the ground, now!"

We raised our hands in the air and ate the pavement.

"This is bullshit!" Nikki shouted.

For the second time in so many days, I was face down on the warm concrete. Steel cuffs slapped around my wrists. This time, it wasn't Sheriff Donnelly or the pretty deputy. It was two others that I hadn't seen before. Wainwright and Pritchard.

"You're under arrest for fighting and disorderly conduct," Wainwright said.

He was a tall blonde guy with a little spare tire. He had that smug, cocky air about him.

"You can't arrest them," Nikki protested. "They didn't do anything. Dusty swung first."

They ignored Nikki and escorted us to the patrol cars.

"You have the right to remain silent..."

They put Jack in one car and me and the other. It looked like we were going to spend the night in jail, compliments of the county.

"I'm gonna get you out," Nikki assured.

20

I f you're looking for a cozy, quiet bed-and-breakfast in the hill country, the Mesquite County jail is not it.

There were a few desks stacked with paperwork. A pot of coffee brewed, filling the air with the stale aroma. No gourmet coffee here. On the far wall, there were pictures of the staff in uniform with the Texas flag in the background. Country music filtered through a small radio. The walls were painted in a pale yellow that had faded and was peeling in parts.

We were put into a central holding tank with one other inmate. The old drunk had pissed himself, and the delightful aroma permeated the cell. There were a few benches, a cold concrete floor, a stainless steel sink and toilet, and a payphone.

It wasn't like this place saw a lot of action. Most of the arrests were for DUI, drunk and disorderly, or some type of petty theft.

The arresting officers filled out paperwork, and a desk clerk answered phones. That was the extent of the night shift.

Nikki showed up at the station, inquiring about getting us out.

Deputy Wainwright told her, "There ain't no way to get them out until they get arraigned in the morning. Nothing you can do until then. Go home, Nikki."

"I'm not going home until you let them out. This is total bullshit, and you know it. Dusty started shit, and they finished it. Why didn't you go after Dusty and them?"

"We'll handle Dusty and his crew."

"You sure showed up awfully fast!"

"We received a call from BB that trouble was brewing outside."

"This ain't fair."

"It is what it is, Nikki."

"It's bullshit. That's what it is. I demand you release them right now. They're sheriff's deputies, you know."

"From another county in another state."

"How about you extend a little professional courtesy?"

"If they wanted courtesy, they shouldn't have come into this county like gangbusters, causing trouble. Now I ain't gonna tell you again. Go home, or I'm going to put you in lock up as well."

"For what?"

"Public intoxication. I can smell it on you. You've been drinking all night."

She scowled at him.

"Go before I hold good to my word."

Nikki glared at him for a moment, then shouted to us across the station. "I'm going to get you out in the morning."

Deputy Wainwright addressed Nikki, "I don't know how you got here, but you better not get in your car and drive home unless you want a DUI."

She glared at him. "You wouldn't dare?"

"Don't tempt me." He paused. "Need me to give you a lift?"

"I wouldn't accept a ride from you if my life depended on it. I'll find my own way home."

Wainwright seemed like a real scumbag. I'm sure he had his eyes on Nikki and thought maybe a ride home would culminate in something else.

JD seethed.

Nikki made a phone call and stepped outside. I figured she was arranging for a ride home.

JD shouted at the deputies, "You boys should come to Coconut County. I can't wait to show you some of our hospitality."

I tried to settle Jack down. Harassing the deputies wasn't going to do us any good. He grumbled under his breath for a few minutes, then finally calmed down.

I tried to make myself comfortable on one of the benches. It was going to be a long night.

21

"You guys have officially moved to the sheriff's bad side," a soft voice said through the iron bars.

Shafts of sunlight filtered through the narrow window in the concrete.

I peeled open my eyes and stirred. My back was sore from the hard bench. I sat up and looked at the pretty blonde deputy as I wiped the sleep from my eyes. I stood up and moved to the bars. The scent of her perfume was refreshing after smelling the sour drunk all night. He burped and farted in his sleep. The sight of Deputy Sawyer made it almost worth it. *Almost.*

"Cream and sugar," I said.

Her face wrinkled. "What?"

"In my coffee, I take cream and sugar."

She laughed. "I'm not getting you a cup of coffee."

I frowned. "What kind of resort is this?"

"It's not a resort."

"How about a ham and cheese omelet?"

"Sorry. You're out of luck."

"I think my luck's starting to change," I said with a smile.

She lifted a curious brow. "Why do you say that?"

"Well, you're going to have breakfast with me after I get out of here."

She laughed again. "What makes you think you're getting out of here?"

"You can't keep us here forever. I may not be familiar with Texas law, but I don't think getting assaulted is a crime. Nobody seems to be bothering with tracking down Dusty and his gang."

"Interesting. They claim you accosted them."

I scoffed. "And the sheriff took their word for it?"

"They *are* local. You *are* a stranger."

We hadn't been processed or printed. Something told me this was pure harassment. There would be no charges.

"I'm not really a stranger anymore. Allow me to formally introduce myself. I'm Deputy Tyson Wild, Coconut County Sheriff's Department."

I extended my hand through the bars.

She hesitated a moment before she accepted the gesture. It was something you would never do with a legitimate inmate. It showed a lot of trust when she took my hand.

She had nice hands. Soft and smooth. Warm. Well manicured. I hung on for a moment as her gaze lingered.

She jerked her hand away as the sheriff burst through the main doors. Sawyer returned to a more hardened stance and stepped away from the bars.

"I see you two just couldn't keep out of trouble," Donnelly said as he stormed toward us.

"Trouble has a way of finding us."

"I see that. You want to tell me what you two are really doing here?"

"I thought that was pretty obvious. We're trying to find out who killed Jim McAllister."

"I heard you talked to Audrey Davis. She gave me a phone call, wanting to know why two out-of-town deputies were questioning her."

"How long have you known Jim McAllister?"

"I'm asking the questions here."

"You don't think it the slightest bit odd that Tiffany got cut completely out of the will?"

Donnelly frowned. He knew it was odd, and he couldn't deny it. "This ain't Florida."

We stared at each other for a long moment.

"You tell Tiffany that I am looking into everything about this case. It may not happen at the pace that she wants it to. But it's a process. These things take time. You know that."

"I think the will was forged," I said.

"That's something for the courts to decide."

"Put a little pressure on Audrey Davis, and her story might change." I told him about the recent deposit to her bank account.

His brow knitted. "Where are you getting your information?"

"I told you. I have sources."

"If you have legitimate sources, provide me with the information. If you acquired this information illegally, it's of no use."

There was a moment of silence.

"I talked to Sheriff Daniels. He told me that despite outward appearances, and a few character flaws, you two are his best deputies."

I smiled with pride.

Donnelly was unamused. "Now, that either means Coconut County is in dire straits, or you morons are actually decent officers."

I feigned modesty. "Well, not to brag, but—"

"Shut it." He frowned and sighed. "Against my better judgment, I'm going to let you two nitwits out. Provided that you promise to leave law enforcement to me and my deputies."

"We're on the same team," I said.

"You two don't much seem like team players."

"I'll leave the law enforcement to you. I've got no problem with that. I could use a vacation. But I'm still gonna ask questions."

Donnelly stared at me for a long moment, then exhaled. "You find anything, you bring it to me, pronto. I don't want you two taking any direct action. You got that?"

I gave him a salute. "Aye-aye, sir."

He glared at me, jingled his keys, and opened the iron gate.

I kicked the bench JD slept on and rousted him. He peeled his eyes open and pulled himself from the bench.

"I'm gonna be keeping a watch on you," Donnelly warned.

Jack smiled as we stepped out of the cell. "Appreciate the hospitality."

Our property was returned, including our badges and pistols.

I looked at Deputy Sawyer. "How about a ride back to the Rattlesnake Saloon?"

She exchanged a glance with the sheriff. He nodded, and Sawyer escorted us out of the station. We climbed into the back of the patrol car.

"You sure you don't want to let me treat you to breakfast?" I said as she drove down the highway.

Her sparkling blue eyes gazed at me in the rearview. "I already had breakfast."

"Then how about lunch?"

22

"I've got plans," Deputy Sawyer said.

"Well, I'm all booked up for dinner. Looks like you missed out."

She laughed. "Did I?"

"Sometimes opportunity only knocks once."

"I guess I'll have to live with regret."

"What's your first name, Deputy?"

"I don't get friendly with inmates."

I feigned offense. "We're not inmates."

She gave me a doubtful glance in the mirror. "Scoundrels. I don't fraternize with scoundrels."

I looked at JD, and we agreed *scoundrels* was acceptable.

"I kinda like that," I said.

Deputy Sawyer rolled her eyes.

She pulled the squad car into the parking lot of the saloon.

The dispatcher crackled over the radio. "Sadie, we got a call that Cletus has climbed the water tower again, bare ass naked. Can you talk him down?"

Sadie radioed back. "I'm on it."

She parked, hopped out, and opened the rear door.

"Thanks for the ride," I said with a smile as I climbed out.

JD followed.

"Stay out of trouble," she said.

"You too."

Sawyer smirked, climbed back into the patrol car, and sped away.

There wasn't much happening at the Rattlesnake Saloon this time of the morning. The parking lot was empty, and the place closed.

Surprisingly, the Porsche was still intact. There were no additional key marks or damage to the vehicle.

I called Tiffany to let her know that we were still alive.

"Oh my God, what happened to you? I've been worried sick!"

I gave her the full story.

"That's ridiculous."

"My thoughts exactly."

"Where are you right now?"

We're at the saloon, picking up the car. I think we're going to grab breakfast, then we'll head back to the ranch."

"Waffle King is good."

"Where's that?"

She gave us directions.

"When I get back, I'll have you make a few phone calls and see if we can get some information from the medical examiner and the Sheriff's Department."

"Okay."

"They should release that information to you upon request. But I'm sure they'll drag their feet about it."

I ended the call, and we drove down the highway to Waffle King. We loaded up on waffles, hash browns, bacon, and coffee, then headed back to the ranch. After spending the night in a drunk tank, I was more than ready for a shower.

After I got cleaned up, I got together with Tiffany and had her call the Medical Examiner's Office. Unlike a large city, Payton Granger picked up the phone right away. Tiffany introduced herself and asked about the autopsy report.

"I haven't finished my report, but I'm more than happy to get you a copy as soon as it's completed," Payton said. "Again, I'm very sorry for your loss."

"Thank you. I'm here with my... *cousin*. He'd like to ask you a few specific questions."

"Certainly."

Tiffany handed the phone to me.

"Have you determined what caliber weapon was used?" I asked.

"That was sent out for ballistics. I probably won't hear back for several weeks. But if I had to hazard a guess, I'd say it was a .30-06. That bullet did a considerable amount of damage. Sorry to be graphic."

"Jim was carrying a .25-06."

"From the trajectory of the entry and exit wound, I would have to say that this was not self-inflicted. This was probably a stray bullet."

"Or an intentional one."

"I guess that's a possibility. All kinds of idiots out there. Somebody could have mistaken him for a deer."

"That seems unlikely."

"It happens all the time."

"I'm sure it does."

I thanked Dr. Granger, then handed the phone back to Tiffany. They chit-chatted for a moment, and she ended the call. I asked her to call Sheriff Donnelly and ask for the release of the crime scene photos.

As I suspected, the request was met with a little resistance.

"You don't want to see those," Donnelly said, his voice cracking through the speaker in the phone.

"Sheriff, I have a right to those images," Tiffany said. "I'd like as much information as I can get my hands on."

"It's not pretty."

"Nothing about this is *pretty*, Sheriff."

"Let me guess who put you up to this."

"Nobody put me up to this."

"Put him on the phone," Donnelly said.

"Who?"

"You know damn good and well who. I know he's standing right there."

Tiffany looked at me and shrugged.

"Howdy, Sheriff," I said.

"What did I tell you about leaving this investigation to local law enforcement?"

"You said not to take any direct action. I promise, whatever information I find, I will pass straight to you and let your department handle it."

"I have your word on that?"

"Absolutely."

He sighed. "Alright. I'll send Deputy Sawyer over with a copy of the file. Don't make me regret this."

"You won't."

I ended the call with a smile and handed the phone back to Tiffany.

"Sounds like a win-win," JD said. "We get the file, and you get to see Deputy Sawyer again."

"Got your eye on her, do you?" Tiffany said with a smile.

"Maybe."

"She's cute. I could see you two together."

"I don't think she sees it that way."

Tiffany laughed. "Maybe she's just playing hard to get."

"Maybe."

23

Deputy Sawyer's patrol car rambled down the dirt road to the house. I guess she had the combination to the gate. She pulled onto the cobblestone drive and parked the car. She exited with a manila folder in hand and climbed the steps to the portico.

Tiffany waited for her at the door.

"You sure you want to take a look at these?" Sawyer asked.

"I'm not gonna look at them," Tiffany said. "He is." She nodded to me.

Sawyer gave me a reluctant look, then handed the folder over.

"Thank you, Sadie," I said.

Her eyes narrowed at me, then flicked to Tiffany. "Did you tell him?"

Tiffany shrugged sheepishly.

"Were you here during the initial response to the incident?" I asked.

She nodded.

"Want to take me out to the scene and walk me through what you saw?"

She paused for a moment, considering it. "I suppose. I've got nothing better to do," she said with a voice full of sarcasm.

I tried to hide my grin. I told Tiffany we'd be back shortly, then followed Sawyer to the patrol car and climbed in front with her.

She gave me a look but didn't say anything.

JD stayed with Tiffany at the house.

The patrol car wasn't exactly suited for off-road, but it handled it well. We made our way out to Widow's Point.

"What do you think about Blair?" I asked.

"I think Blair is *Blair*."

"Care to elaborate?"

"I think Blair saw an opportunity, and she took it."

"So you think she married Jim for his money?"

"Maybe there was something more between them, maybe there wasn't. Who am I to say?"

"What do you think about the situation with the will?"

"It's a little surprising, but maybe Jim's last wishes were to give everything to his new bride."

"Of six months?"

"You think she killed him?" Sadie asked.

"I don't think she pulled the trigger, but she certainly has the most to gain."

"Look, the sheriff interviewed her, Cole, Tiffany, Earl, and everyone remotely involved. He didn't get the sense that any of those people had anything to do with this."

"Some people are good liars." I paused. "How many homicides do you see in this county a year?"

"A year?" she scoffed. "Maybe one a decade. There hasn't been a homicide around here since..."

"So, admittedly, this isn't your forte."

"Mesquite County is not what I would call a high crime area."

"Don't take this the wrong way, but your department just doesn't have the experience to deal with this kind of thing."

She gave me an annoyed look, then admitted, "You're right. We don't. But we're doing the best we can." She paused. "I think this is a lot simpler than you're making it out to be. I think Jim was out on the property, stumbled across somebody who didn't belong, something happened, and Jim wound up with a bullet in him. I think whoever did this is long gone."

"What do you know about drug trafficking in the area?"

"I know that people are bringing it up from the border. Sometimes you have people carrying it all the way up here in backpacks, a few kilos at a time. But we really don't see much of that. If they are moving through the territory, it's usually at night, and they're in and out."

We arrived at the trail that led to Widow's Point. Sadie parked the car, and we hopped out and walked the path to the location of the incident.

The sun was high in the sky, and it baked the ground with its incessant rays. Birds fluttered in the trees. Every now and then, a hot breeze drifted across the treacherous landscape.

We reached the site where Jim had been killed.

"What do you remember about the scene?" I asked.

"It was after dark when I got here. Jim's body was here," she said, pointing to a spot near the blood spatter.

"Has anyone been over to Earl's place to look for shell casings?"

"No."

"Why not?"

She didn't have an answer.

I walked around the area, looking for anything. Finding a casing out here would be next to impossible.

I pointed to the fence line. "He was clearly shot from this direction."

A gunshot rang out, echoing across the terrain.

It snapped through the air, whizzing past my ear.

I grabbed Sadie and tackled her to the ground.

Another gunshot snapped overhead.

24

"**S**tay down," I said, drawing my pistol, scanning the area.

"Get off me!" Sadie growled.

We huddled behind a boulder, hugging the dirt, the scrub brush somewhat obscuring us from the shooter.

"You hit?"

"No," she replied.

Sadie radioed dispatch. "Shots fired! I need backup at the McAllister ranch. We're at Widow's Point."

"Still think Jim's shooter was transient?" I muttered.

It was silent except for the wind.

I peered over the boulder and scanned the horizon. A well-camouflaged sniper would be hard to see in this terrain. For a moment, I saw nothing.

Then movement gave away his position.

The shooter hightailed it out of the area, heading north and disappearing into the brush.

He wore a ghillie suit—the ultimate way to blend in with the terrain, popular with military snipers. Designed to meld seamlessly with the environment, it was a collage of synthetic foliage and fabric strips. Each piece a different tone and texture. Untamed randomness that mimicked the organic asymmetry of the terrain. Wisps of material hung from the suit like moss. Without movement, you could look right at a sniper in a ghillie suit and never see him.

As the shooter ran away, he looked like some type of monster.

"He's heading toward Cooter's place," I said.

"Doesn't mean the shooter was Cooter," Sadie replied.

We climbed from the ground and brushed the dirt off. I looked myself over and surveyed Sadie. Sometimes adrenaline can mask the pain of an injury, and there was a lot of it coursing through our veins.

We hustled back down the path to the patrol car. Sadie slid behind the wheel and contacted dispatch again.

She took a moment to settle her nerves.

"Take a deep breath. We're okay."

She inhaled, held it, then breathed out slowly.

"First time you've been shot at?" I asked.

"Yeah. That kind of thing doesn't happen around here. Hopefully, it's the last time."

My heart still thumped my chest. I knew hers had to be pumping.

"I'm not going to say it ever gets normal, but you learn to handle the rush."

Adrenaline, like any other drug, could be addictive. I knew plenty of guys that, after a while, began to crave contact with the enemy. Normal life just couldn't move the needle in the same way.

Sadie drove back toward the main house.

By the time we neared the estate, the sheriff had arrived. He climbed out of his vehicle and waited for us to pull into the driveway.

"What the hell is going on?" he asked as we climbed out of the patrol car.

Sadie gave him the rundown.

His face tightened. "Are you okay?"

"I'm fine," she replied.

"I'm okay, too," I added, just to be annoying.

He glared at me.

"Did you get a look at the shooter?"

Sadie shook her head. "Tyson did."

"He was in a full camouflage ghillie suit," I said.

I told him the direction the shooter ran off in, then updated him with my theory about the affair between Jim and Brooke Barnes.

"I'll have a talk with Cooter, see if he's seen anyone on his property."

A frown tensed my face. "I'm thinking Cooter may have been the shooter."

"I'm having a hard time believing that," Donnelly said. "But I'll look into it."

"I'd like to look into it with you."

"He's right, Sheriff," Sadie said. "If Brooke was having an affair with Jim, Cooter may have let jealousy get the best of him." Then she added, "And Cooter was a sniper in the Marine Corps."

"I've known Cooter Barnes for a long time, and I don't think he's crazy enough to take a shot at you. He knows who he'd have to deal with," Donnelly said to Deputy Sawyer.

I began to think there was a little more to their relationship, though he was quite a bit older.

Tiffany and Blair emerged from the house with JD.

"We heard gunshots," Tiffany said. "Are you okay?"

I told them the situation.

There was someone conspicuously missing from the group. "Where's Cole?"

"I don't know. I haven't seen him in a while."

"He told me he was heading to the South Crossing to fill feeders," Blair said.

We'd been shot at from the north, but that didn't mean much.

Cole's Raptor rambled down the dirt road, spitting gravel and kicking up dust. He pulled onto the driveway and hopped out with a concerned look on his face. "What's going on?"

"Where have you been?" I asked in an accusatory tone.

"At the South Crossing, why?"

"Somebody just tried to kill us, that's all," I snarked.

Cole's eyes rounded. "I heard a gunshot. Two, actually."

"Mind if we take a look in your truck?"

Sheriff Donnelly gave me a look but didn't stop me.

"No," Cole said, confused. "Why?"

I moved to the Raptor without explaining myself. I pulled open the door and scanned the cab.

There were no weapons inside.

I looked in the bed of the truck.

Just bags of feed.

Then I checked his toolbox.

Nothing out of the ordinary.

No ghillie suit anywhere in the truck.

He could have easily dumped the items. He had enough time to shoot from Earl's property, then hightail it around to the south side, hop in his truck, and return. But he would need to have been moving at a pretty good pace. The timing was tight.

I stepped away from the truck and rejoined the group. I told the sheriff I'd like to speak with Earl and look around the property where the incident occurred.

To my surprise, Donnelly didn't put up a fight.

JD and I hopped into the patrol car with Deputy Sawyer, and we followed the sheriff next door to Earl's ranch. Sadie was still a little shaken by the event. Her hands jittered as she dropped the car into gear and took the wheel.

Earl's gate was open, and we pulled onto the property and drove up to the main house. Sadie recognized his truck, so we figured he was home.

The terrain was more of the same, and lazy cows lounged, taking shade under tall oaks. The old white house had a large veranda and peeling white paint.

We hopped out of the vehicles and climbed the steps to the veranda. The sheriff put a heavy fist against the door, and Earl answered a moment later with a curious look on his face. He didn't like seeing us at his door. "What's this about?"

"You hear gunshots?" Donnelly asked.

"I did. Sounded like they came from the southwest side, near Widow's Point."

"Have you been out that way?" I asked.

"Nope. Been at the house all morning."

"The shots came from your property."

His eyes narrowed at me. "How do you figure that?"

"I saw the shooter."

He lifted his bushy brows.

"Somebody just took potshots at Deputy Sawyer and Deputy Wild," Donnelly said.

I was a little surprised that the sheriff used my title.

Concern tensed Earl's face. "You're saying those shots came from my property?"

"Yes, sir," I replied.

"You own a ghillie suit?" Sadie asked.

"I do. Why?"

"You want to show it to us?"

His face tightened. "It's nothing special. But if you want to take a look at it, be my guest. I got it in the closet here."

He turned from the door and hobbled down the foyer with a distinct limp.

"You hurt yourself?" Sheriff Donnelly asked.

"I twisted my dang knee this morning. Not really sure what the hell I did. It swelled up, so I've just been taking it easy."

Earl moved to a closet in the foyer and reached inside.

We were all a little jumpy, and the sheriff put his hand on the grip of his pistol, just in case Earl decided to pull a surprise out of the closet. I did the same. The closet door blocked our view.

25

Earl pulled out the camouflage suit. The stringy tendrils made the wearer look like some kind of swamp monster. There were varying degrees of craftsmanship from suit to suit and brand to brand, but they all pretty much looked the same from a distance. I couldn't be certain that this was the same suit.

I wasn't familiar with Earl's physical capabilities. I didn't know how fast he could run or just how maneuverable he was. But from my brief glimpse of the shooter, he was quick. That didn't quite match Earl's current condition. It's quite possible that running away from the scene of the incident caused him to tweak his knee.

If his injury was genuine, he wouldn't be doing any running now.

"What kind of weapons do you own?" I asked.

"I got shotguns, rifles, pistols, and a few black powder rifles."

"You own a .30-06?"

"I do." He exhaled a frustrated breath, and his eyes narrowed at me again. "I'm not sure what the point of this is."

"You mind if we take a look around your property?" Sheriff Donnelly asked.

"Knock yourself out, Sheriff."

"You want to take us out to the fence line at Widow's Point?"

Earl sighed, "I reckon."

He hobbled out of the foyer and onto the veranda. He grabbed the railing as he climbed down the creaky wooden steps and shuffled to his truck. It was an old red and white Chevy with a fair amount of rust. He climbed in, and the door creaked, then clanged as he pulled it shut. The engine rumbled as he cranked it up, and we hopped back into the patrol cars.

Earl led us down a dirt path to the southwest side of his property. When we had gone as far as the road would allow, we climbed out, and Earl pointed us in the direction. "You don't mind if I sit this one out. I'm not inclined to tackle the terrain today."

JD stayed behind and kept Earl company.

Earl didn't look too pleased about that.

We marched along the rocky, uneven ground, through the craggy bushes, cedar, and mesquite trees to a clearing by the fence line that bordered Widow's Point to the south.

During the shooting, I had tried my best to find landmarks to identify the shooter's position as he scampered off. All the terrain looked similar out here, and it was hard to pinpoint the location from this side of the fence. I finally settled on an area. "I think the shooter was right about here."

From where I stood, there was a direct line of sight to the trail where we had been standing and where Jim had been shot. It was as good a vantage point as any. There was a low boulder that offered a perfect shooting position with a little bit of cover. A clear trail to the northwest allowed exfiltration. Then the terrain sloped down to a valley. There were plenty of trees to cover the escape route.

We searched the area, looking for shell casings. It took about 15 minutes of scouring the ground, but we came up with two shell casings from a .30-06.

The sheriff snapped on a pair of gloves, collected the evidence, and bagged them. "I'll send these off to the lab, but it's gonna take a while."

"Have them check for fingerprints and markings from the firing pin. We may be able to match that to a weapon, if we can find the weapon."

"I'll talk to Earl and see if he wants to voluntarily submit his rifle. If not, I'll go about getting a warrant."

I was glad to see the sheriff on board for a change.

We returned to Earl, and the sheriff laid it out for him. I was pretty sure Earl wouldn't be too keen on handing over his rifle.

26

W e left Earl's property and headed to speak to Cooter Barnes. The sheriff had called him and told him we were coming. Cooter gave him the combination to the gate, and we pulled onto the property without any trouble. Cooter waited for us at the front door. We hopped out of the patrol cars and climbed the steps to the veranda.

Cooter greeted the sheriff with a handshake. "What can I do for you?"

Cooter was late 50s with narrow blue eyes, tan skin, and a weathered face. His brown hair was starting to sprout bits of gray on the sides. It was receding at the corners and thinning at the peak. He didn't seem mean or ornery.

"Can you tell me where you've been this morning?" Sheriff Donnelly asked.

"Well, I got up early and went into town and picked up some supplies. I came back and mowed the grass around the house before it got too hot, then I came in for lunch. I figure

I'll wait till it cools off a little bit before I go out and fill the feeders."

"You haven't been over to Earl's property, have you?"

Cooter's brow knitted. "No. I don't have much to do with Earl. We're friendly and all. But..."

"You own a ghillie suit?"

"I do, but I almost never use it."

"You got a .30-06, don't you?"

"I do," Cooter said, growing concerned. "What's this about?"

The sheriff told him.

Cooter's narrow eyes rounded. "That happened today?"

"Little over an hour ago now."

"I hope you don't think I had anything to do with that. I was right here. I mean, what possible reason would I have to take shots at the deputies? Hell, I've known Sadie since she was shitting diapers."

Sadie huffed and gave him a look.

"Sorry. But it's true. You was the cutest little baby, too." He smiled.

"Is Brooke home?" Donnelly asked.

Cooter frowned. "No." He took a deep breath. "Truth be told, she left me. She's living with Darlene for the time being."

"That wouldn't have anything to do with her relationship with Jim McAllister, would it?"

The muscles in Cooter's jaw flexed. "I don't feel like discussing my personal business, Sheriff."

"Well, you can discuss it here or at the station."

Cooter gave the sheriff a surprised look. "You arresting me?"

"I'm telling you that you need to start answering questions. Now it's my understanding Brooke may have been having some sort of affair with Jim McAllister. The fact she's not living with you anymore leads me to believe those rumors might be true. Now, I've known you for a long time, and I think you're a pretty easygoing guy. But sometimes passion gets the best of us. Somebody shot Jim McAllister, and somebody shot at these two deputies. The shooter was on Earl's property and he headed in your direction afterward. Be transparent with me, and we can move on to the next suspect."

Cooter's eyes narrowed and flicked between all of us. He hesitated a moment, then exhaled. "I'm pretty damn sure she was involved with McAllister. I don't know the extent of it, but I know that her heart wasn't here anymore."

"Did that make you mad?" I asked.

"You're damn right. I'd be lying if I said I didn't think about putting a bullet in that son-of-a-bitch. Excuse my language. But I did not traipse across Earl's property and shoot Jim McAllister, nor did I shoot at these two deputies. I'd never do something like that. And if I did, I wouldn't miss."

"How about you hand over your rifle?" Donnelly said.

"Which one?"

"The .30-06. And let's see that ghillie suit, too."

27

"I'm gonna get that back, ain't I?" Cooter asked.

"You'll get it back," Sheriff Donnelly assured. "Provided it's clean."

Cooter had shown us his ghillie suit. It looked like every other that I had seen.

The sheriff took the rifle and put it in the trunk with Earl's.

"That ain't what I'd use," Cooter shouted from the porch.

"What would you use?" the sheriff asked.

"My Remington 700."

That didn't surprise me. The M40 used by the Marines, since replaced by the MK13, was based on the Remington 700. Cooter would have been intimately familiar with the weapon. Then again, maybe he used something else to throw off suspicion.

I hopped into the patrol car with Deputy Sawyer, and JD rode with the sheriff. We drove back to the McAllister ranch.

I called Isabella along the way. "I need you to track cell phones for Cooter Barnes and Earl Jackson. Let me know if you can put those devices anywhere near Widow's Point this morning, or at the time of Jim McAllister's murder."

"I'll see what I can do."

I ended the call and slipped the phone back into my pocket.

The interaction had drawn a curious gaze from Sadie. "Who is that?"

"My source."

"Sounds convenient. I wish we had something like that. It takes forever to get anything accomplished around here."

We pulled onto the property at Jim's and drove up to the house.

Sadie put the patrol car in park, and I sat in the passenger seat for a moment.

"What are your plans for the rest of the day?" I asked.

"I already told you I don't have lunch with scoundrels," she teased with a slight grin.

"And I told you, that ship sailed. I'm not asking again."

"I didn't figure you for a quitter?" She tried not to smile but didn't do a good job of it.

I may have smiled too. "I'm no quitter. Take that to the bank."

"Time will tell," she said.

"I've been thinking about Gracie Hutchins."

"And what are you thinking?"

"I think she's at the bottom of Coyote Canyon Lake. But the sheriff didn't seem too interested in sending out a dive team."

"We don't have a dive team."

"Her cell phone puts her near Buzzard's Roost the night of her disappearance. I figure somebody may have seen something."

"You want to go down to Buzzard's Roost and ask around?"

I grinned. "Are you asking me to lunch?"

She rolled her eyes. "No. I'm not asking you to lunch. But they do have good food."

"It's a date," I said. "We could stop by and talk to Haley Hutchins's boyfriend along the way."

"You think he had some involvement in Gracie's disappearance?"

"From what I hear of him, it wouldn't surprise me."

"Well, Wade Larkin doesn't have the best reputation around town. And the sheriff did want me to keep an eye on you two. This is as good a way as any."

JD hopped out of the sheriff's car, and I rolled down the window and waved him over. "Get in. We got work to do."

He grinned and climbed into the backseat.

28

Weeds sprouted around an old, rusted-out 1950 Chevy truck. The original green paint was barely visible. You couldn't tell where the grass ended, and the vehicle began. It didn't have any tires. It just sat on blocks. It made a hell of a lawn ornament.

It may have been the best-looking thing on the property.

A single-wide trailer that was almost as overgrown as the vehicle sat on a narrow strip of land. The weeds snaked in and out of the latticework at the base of the trailer. Creaky wooden steps, faded and sun-bleached, led up to the front door.

The trailer had rust spots, and in general, the area hadn't been well maintained. But amid all of that, there was a shiny black F-150 with big polished tires and aggressive graphics. It was easy to see where Wade's priorities were.

Then again, this wasn't his trailer.

It belonged to Haley Hutchins. I suspected that Wade was living here rent-free. I'm not sure how he afforded the truck. Sadie said he didn't have steady employment. He picked up odd jobs here and there.

Sadie pulled up to the trailer, and we hopped out. I let JD out of the back, and we approached the home. We climbed the steps, and Sadie put a fist against the door.

Window panes rattled.

I'm sure whoever was inside heard us approach.

Footsteps stomped across the trailer, and the blinds in the window moved. A moment later, a man shouted through the door, "What do you want?"

"We'd like to have a word with you, Wade," Sadie shouted through the door.

"What's this about?"

"We're trying to find Gracie, if you give a care?"

There was a moment of silence, then he pulled open the door and looked at us with a scowl.

Wade was about 6'1" with a narrow face, sunken cheeks, dull blue eyes, and wavy brown hair that was almost blond from the sun at the tips. He wasn't the kind of guy to get highlights.

The sun had done a number on his skin over the years, and I put him in his mid-30s. He was a wiry guy, and I figured he had a lot of fight in him. He smelled like an ashtray.

A glance behind him, into the trailer, told me he didn't care much for housekeeping. The only thing he gave a shit about was that truck.

"Sheriff Donnelly's already been out here asking questions," Wade said. "I told him everything I know."

His eyes were bloodshot, and I figured he was pretty well into it, even at this hour.

"When was the last time you saw Gracie?" I asked.

He glared at me. "Who the hell are you?"

"They're a special crimes unit," Sadie said, not bothering to add that we had no jurisdiction.

I appreciated the gesture.

"What's so special about this crime?" Wade asked. "Do you even know that there's been a crime? I'm telling you, that little twit ran off. She's probably soaking up the sun on a California beach right now, laughing her ass off while everyone around here is chasing their tails."

"I don't think she's in California," I said.

"Why is that?"

"Her cell records indicate that she was picked up along the highway and taken to Coyote Canyon Lake."

"So, she's at the lake?"

"Could be."

"Well, maybe that's where you should look for her." He didn't seem to care one way or another if Gracie ever came back.

Needless to say, I didn't like the guy.

"Can you tell me where you were the night of Gracie's disappearance?"

His brow knitted. "I already told the sheriff that I was at home with her mother."

"Is her mother here now?"

"No, she's not."

"You know where she is?"

"I'm not her keeper."

"Is Maddie here?"

"Maddie ain't here, neither."

"What was your relationship like with Gracie?" I asked.

"What kind of question is that?"

"Did you get along?

"Both those girls have an attitude. You try living in a house with three crazy bitches. Tell me how you'd like it. I think I deserve an award for putting up with them."

"Did you ever have to discipline those kids?"

He scoffed. "Hell, you gotta discipline every kid."

"Did you ever get physical with them?"

He glared at me. "You don't have kids, do you?"

I shook my head.

"I try to be a good role model for them, but I think those girls are beyond my help."

Sadie stifled an eye-roll.

Wade Larkin was the farthest thing in the world from a good role model.

"You ever hit Gracie or Maddie?" I asked.

His glare persisted. "I thought you was looking for Gracie."

"We are. I'm just trying to get an idea of the dynamic."

"Dynamic?"

"I'm just wondering if the girls felt safe."

His jaw tightened. "I'm gonna tell you the same thing I told those bastards from CPS. I never laid a hand on those kids. I put up with their bullshit. I gave them money here and there. And what do I get for it? Nothing." He exhaled a frustrated breath. "Protective services came out here twice. Asked the girls all kinds of questions. Asked me questions. Asked Haley questions. They found no indication of impropriety. And I don't appreciate you coming out here and raising those allegations again."

"Nobody's making any allegations."

"Right, *just asking questions*," he mocked.

"Did Gracie have a boyfriend?"

"I don't keep up with the love life of those little sluts. Wouldn't surprise me if they're out there selling their asses."

I really didn't like this guy.

"Maddie sure is cute," I said, egging him on.

"Damn right she is. Another year and she'll be ripe."

Sadie tried to contain a shiver.

"Actually, in Texas, 17s legal," Sadie said.

He looked impressed. "Is that so?"

"Don't get any funny ideas, Wade."

"She's practically my stepdaughter. I'd no more look at her that way as I would a child."

I had more than a few reservations about Wade.

"Why don't you ask Maddie? She'll tell you. I never treated either of those kids poorly."

"See, I'm thinking that you weren't here that night," I said. "I think you were out drinking. You saw her along the road and offered her a ride home. Maybe you got a funny idea. Then something went wrong, and she wound up dead. I think she's at the bottom of the lake, and I think you know exactly where she is."

Wade's face tightened, and his cheeks flushed. "That's a bold statement. Anything to back it up?"

"Give it time. I will."

He laughed. "I think it's time you all get off my property." He stepped inside and slammed the door.

Window panes rattled.

Sadie muttered. "You like to get under people's skin, don't you?"

"It's a special skill," I said with a grin.

We plunged down the creaky steps and walked back to the patrol car.

Wade watched from the window.

We climbed in, left the property, and headed down to the Buzzard's Roost.

29

There was no better place to spend a hot Texas day in Mesquite County than Coyote Canyon Lake.

A few days away from the ocean, I was starting to feel landlocked.

This wasn't exactly the teal waves of the Florida Keys, but it was as close as I was going to get. The lake water was more of an emerald green. Boats skimmed across the surface, pulling skiers. Scantily clad beauties found themselves on foredecks. You weren't going to find many superyachts around here, but there were plenty of 27-foot and 35-foot speedboats, center consoles, and wake boats. There was the occasional sailboat.

There was a decent size marina at the Buzzard's Roost, along with a boat ramp. The restaurant had an outdoor deck, and the shade offered some respite from the sun. The place was packed. People ate, drank beer, and socialized. Boaters on the lake could cruise right up to the Buzzard's Roost, tie off, and have lunch.

We pulled into the parking lot and hopped out. I glanced around, surveying the scene, taking a look at the boat ramp and the marina.

We stepped inside the restaurant, and the smell of grilled food swirled—cheeseburgers, chicken sandwiches, fajitas, quesadillas, fried shrimp, po' boys, you name it.

A cheery blonde hostess asked, "Table for three?"

I nodded.

"Inside or out?"

I looked at my companions, and Sadie said, "Inside."

The hostess escorted us to a table, weaving through the crowd. Forks clicked against plates, and the murmur of conversation drifted about.

The hostess led us to our table, and we took our seats. She passed out menus and told us to enjoy our meal. Our server would be with us shortly.

I told Sadie I was going to talk to the bartender and excused myself.

"I'll go with you."

"I'll hold down the fort," JD said, perusing the menu.

We made our way to the bar and leaned against the counter. It didn't take long to get the bartender's attention. Sadie waved Deborah over. She was in her mid-30s with brown hair, brown eyes, and a splattering of freckles on her face. When she wasn't behind the bar, she was out on the lake, and her skin told the story.

Deborah smiled. "What can I do for you, deputy?"

"It's about Gracie Hutchins."

Deborah frowned. "I hope the poor girl is okay. Between you and me, I think Wade had a hand in that."

"You and I are on the same page," I said.

Sadie introduced me. We shook hands and exchanged pleasantries.

"We believe that Gracie was abducted and taken down here the night she disappeared. I'm wondering if you may have seen something. It would have been around 1:00 AM."

"I'm usually dayshift. But if I recall, we closed at midnight that night."

"Why?"

"That was a Monday. Mondays are always slow here. We shut down anywhere between 11:00 PM and midnight, depending on the crowd." Deborah paused. "You might want to talk to Brad." She looked at her watch. "He should be here around 5:00 PM." She paused and, in a solemn tone, said, "You think she was taken to the lake and...?"

I nodded.

"Are you thinking she's still at the lake?" Deborah asked, knowing what my response would be.

"Unfortunately. But we don't have anything conclusive."

We'd burned most of the day with our previous interviews. 5:00 PM wasn't terribly far away. I figured it was time for me to call Maddie. With us asking questions, she'd hear about it sooner or later, especially in a town like this.

"I can put the word out," Deborah said. "Maybe somebody saw something. Maddie came in here not long ago, putting up flyers. I don't think she's gotten a response from them yet."

"Get in touch with me if you hear anything," Sadie said.

"Yes, ma'am," Deborah said.

We returned to the table, and Deborah returned to her customers. I tried to call Maddie, but I couldn't get cell service here.

"If you were going to dump a body, where would it be?" I asked Sadie.

"It's a big lake. I'd weigh her down and dump her in the deepest part."

"Where's that?"

30

We watched people have a good time on the lake and chowed down on a late lunch that rolled into Happy Hour. I went with the Buzzard Chicken Wrap, filled with marinated chicken, romaine lettuce, cherry tomatoes, avocado, all rolled up into a flour tortilla with cilantro and lime. JD ordered the Lone Star Shrimp Po' Boy—Gulf shrimp on a baguette with zesty sauce, lettuce, and ripe tomatoes. Sadie opted for the pulled pork sliders.

I hadn't had a bad meal yet in this town, and this one didn't disappoint.

"I've got some equipment ordered. Should be here tomorrow," JD said. "I say we take out Tiffany's boat and see what we can find."

I told Sadie she should tag along.

"Well, I am supposed to be keeping an eye on you. And a day out on the lake sounds better than a day in a patrol car. Especially in this heat."

"Careful," JD said. "He might start to think you like hanging around us."

"Like might be a strong word," she said. "Tolerate. I'm tolerating you both at this point."

JD rolled his eyes.

We decided to order some Snakebite Ale. It was almost mandatory. The waitress brought us a few bottles of the amber longnecks. JD and I clinked glasses and sipped the zesty beverage. Cold sweat beaded on the bottle.

Sadie looked on with envy.

"What time do you get off duty?"

"Technically, I'm off at 5:00 PM today. But I can't drink in uniform."

"Get out of the uniform," I said in a slightly lascivious tone.

She gave me a look. "You're not getting that lucky."

"Look at all these ladies running around in skimpy bikinis. How much different can it be than underwear?"

"You want me to strip down to my skivvies right here?"

"If you insist."

She scoffed. "How do you know I'm wearing underwear?"

She had piqued my curiosity.

"Stop visualizing me in my underwear."

"I'm not. You said you weren't wearing any."

She rolled her eyes. "I'm not sure I'm safe on a boat with you two tomorrow."

"You've got a gun."

"True. And I know how to use it."

We hung out for a few beers and took advantage of the Happy Hour specials. 5:00 PM turned into 6:00 PM, then 7:00 PM. The amber ball had plunged over the hills. It cooled off somewhat, but not nearly enough.

The Snakebite Ale wasn't bad. It hit the spot. Good music cranked from the jukebox, and there was a lively crowd.

My phone buzzed with a call from Isabella. "I found your girls."

"Really? Where are they?"

"Well, you're not going to like this. Penny's dead."

"What!?"

"She was drunk, went off the road, and hit a tree. Outskirts of Austin."

"When did that happen?"

"A few days ago."

"What about Savannah?"

"She goes by Savvy Redd on For the Fans. You'd like her content. I'll send you a link."

"Where's she at?"

"LA County morgue."

A deflated sigh escaped my mouth.

"Talk about Karma…"

"At this point, I'm not convinced they were even present for the signing," I said. "Blair could have forged their signatures and paid off Audrey."

"Anything's possible." In a hurried voice, she said, "Gotta run. We'll talk soon."

I ended the call and updated JD and Sadie.

It wasn't too long after when Nikki arrived on a 25-foot sport boat with a couple friends. They'd been out on the lake all day and looked a little tipsy.

Nikki wore a delightful string bikini, and she had some intriguing tan lines. The taut fabric hugged her form, barely able to contain fleshy mounds of goodness. It looked like a wardrobe malfunction was imminent. With each movement, the fabric struggled to contain her perkiness, but somehow the bikini held on. She spotted JD, sauntered over to our table, and fell into his lap.

"I see you got yourself out of jail."

"We were granted clemency," JD said with a grin, his mood elevated by her presence.

"I called in the morning, but they said you had already been released."

"I'd have given you a call, but you never gave me your number."

She surveyed him carefully. "I guess that's true. We always get interrupted."

"It seems that way."

"Maybe that's the Universe trying to keep us apart."

"Maybe that's the Universe testing us, trying to see how much we want it," JD said.

"And how much do you want it, Sugar?" she asked with a naughty tone and smoldering eyes.

Deputy Sawyer rolled her eyes. "Should we give you two some privacy?"

"He ain't earned it yet," Nikki said. "But he's on his way."

Jack smiled.

Nikki waved over her friends and introduced us to Faith and her boyfriend, Dwayne. They knew Sadie.

"Come on the boat with us," Nikki said to Jack.

He gave us a look.

"Go ahead," I said.

"I'll make sure you get home safe," Nikki said.

"Adventure awaits," JD replied with an eager grin.

Nikki looked at Sadie. "You guys can come too. There's plenty of room."

"No, thank you," Sadie said.

"Oh, live a little! When was the last time you had some fun?"

"I have fun all the time," Sadie said, a little tense.

"I'm talking about real fun, Deputy Sawyer. You don't have to be a cop all the time."

"Goes with the job."

"All that stress isn't good for you. Let your hair down. Relax."

I'm not going to say that Sadie was uptight. But she was squared away. I got the impression that she didn't drink much, didn't smoke, certainly didn't do drugs, and kept her wits about herself at all times. She didn't strike me as the type to cut loose and throw caution to the wind. She had a reserved quality about her.

"I really should be getting home," Sadie said.

"It's early," Nikki said. "Hell, it's not even 8:00 o'clock yet. Plenty of time to get in trouble."

Sadie chuckled. "I'm trying to keep these two *out* of trouble. We've had enough for today."

Nikki shrugged. "Suit yourself." She looked at JD. "You coming?"

It was a loaded question.

"Wouldn't miss it." He pushed away from the table and started to dig into his wallet.

"I'll pick up the check," I said.

"Much obliged," he replied, putting a little twang in his voice. "Don't wait up."

I laughed.

Sadie urged me to "Go! Have fun with your friends."

"I'm having fun right here."

Sadie tried not to smile, but I noticed a small one.

"Oh, don't be a stick in the mud!" Nikki said as they walked away.

"It's just a boat ride," I said.

"I'll have you back in no time," Nikki assured.

"How much trouble can we really get in?" I said.

Sadie gave me a grave look. Around here, there was a world of trouble to get into.

31

The engines howled, and the smell of exhaust swirled as the twin outboards spit a frothy wake. We carved through the inky surface of the lake that was like glass now. A few lights dotted the hillside, but it wasn't developed out here. Lots of wide open spaces. In 30 years, this could be a resort town. But now, it was small and quiet, and that's just the way most people liked it.

There was no briny air. No mists of saltwater. We cruised out to the middle of the lake, and Dwayne cut the engine. The boat slumped in the swells, and we drifted for a moment, all alone in the obsidian blackness.

Classic rock pumped through speakers, and Nikki passed out a round of brew for everyone, including Sadie.

"No, thank you," the deputy replied.

"Ain't nobody gonna see you out here," Nikki assured.

"That's okay. I still have to drive home in a patrol car after this."

"It's not like you're going to get pulled over."

"If I did, Sheriff Donnelly would have my ass. I'd never live that down."

Nikki gave her a look. "I can see this is going to be a project. It's gonna take time. But I'm going to teach you how to have fun, if it's the last thing I do."

Nikki seemed to be an expert on the subject. At least, her brand of fun.

The couples on the boat paired off, and it wasn't long before JD and Nikki were locking lips.

There was an awkward moment between Sadie and me. The implied peer pressure was strong.

"Don't get any funny ideas. I'm not that easy."

I raised my hands innocently. "It's cute that you think I want to kiss you."

She lifted an astonished eyebrow and feigned offense.

"I'm perfectly happy sipping my beer and enjoying the moonlight."

The moon glowed over the water, speckling the ripples in the lake. A bazillion stars flickered overhead. It had cooled off a little, and the slight breeze kept it from being unbearable. Though it was still sweltering.

Jack and Nikki broke for air.

Nikki said, "I'm hot."

"That you are," JD agreed.

Nikki smirked and stood up. "I mean the weather. It's still hot." She changed the station and put on some pop music. She sauntered back toward JD, then reached a hand behind her back and tugged ever so slowly on the knot in her bikini top. It didn't take a genius to know where this was going, but she drew it out just to extend the anticipation of it. Finally, after an eternity, the knot snapped free, and the fabric went slack. The top still covered her perky peaks while she untied the knot around her neck, then held the bikini in place with her forearms before letting it fall away.

Her magnificence jiggled.

Beautiful orbs in the pale moonlight.

JD was hypnotized.

"Who's going skinny-dipping with me?"

JD raised his hand discreetly.

Nikki giggled.

"I knew it wouldn't take long for this to turn into the Prancing Pony," Sadie muttered.

Nikki shot her a look. "Would you quit being a stick in the mud? Besides, if you get out of that uniform, you might be able to have a beer."

One at a time, with all the dramatics of a burlesque performer, Nikki untied the bow on one hip and then on the other, and her bikini bottom fell away, revealing the promised land. She had the cutest little landing strip, and I didn't think JD would need a Landing Signal Officer to guide him in.

She moved to the gunwale and dove into the water. She plunged below and surfaced an instant later, slinging the water from her hair, combing it back across her scalp. "Feels great. You coming in?"

"Don't have to ask me twice," JD said.

It didn't take him long to get into his birthday suit, and I averted my eyes. That was something I didn't need to see.

Dwayne and Faith joined them.

"You know there are alligators in there," Sadie said just to get a rise out of them.

"No, there's not," Nikki replied.

It was rare to see an alligator this far west.

"Go ahead and join them," Sadie said to me.

"I don't want to be the odd man out."

"You don't have to get naked," Nikki shouted. "Just go swimming in your underwear. What's the difference?"

"Oh, no. If the sheriff heard about this, I'd be in deep trouble."

"What happens on this boat stays on this boat," Nikki said. "Ain't that right?"

Everyone agreed.

"I'm not trying to get you naked," I said. "But what's the harm with a little swim?"

She gave me a look. "You want me to give you a list?"

I grinned. "Do you really care if Sheriff Donnelly hears about you on a boat having fun on the lake? It's not like he's your father."

"He is her father," Nikki shouted with a mouthful of water as she treaded.

I lifted a surprised brow. "I thought there was something between you two."

"A Donnelly has been sheriff in this town for the last several hundred years," Nikki said.

"Quite a legacy," I said, impressed.

"Holister Donnelly brought down the Blackwood Bandits in 1879 after the great train robbery of Mesquite County."

I gave Sadie an impressed glance. "That's quite the reputation. Why the name change? You're not married, are you?"

She sneered at me. "No. I took my mother's maiden name. I didn't want to live off my father's reputation."

"A trailblazer. Wanted to make your own name?"

"I didn't want people to think I got the position just because I was his daughter."

"It seems everybody in town knows you're his daughter."

"Still. There's a difference. When I go by Sawyer, it's a statement. I'm standing on my own. And I told my father he hires and fires me based on merit alone. I don't want a handout."

"You seem pretty self-sufficient to me."

"You're damn right. And I intend to stay that way."

"Did somebody say train robbery?" JD asked.

"Yes," Nikki said. "One of the biggest in Texas. They say the gold is still in the hills somewhere around Snakebite."

"Nobody knows for sure," Sadie said. "It's probably a myth."

"Only a few pieces of gold were ever recovered," Nikki said.

"Now this I gotta hear," I said.

"Not much to tell. Beau Blackwood and his gang robbed the train. There was a standoff in the hills at Iron Horse Junction. It ended in a shootout with the sheriff. The members of the Blackwood gang were killed, and Beau Blackwood was hung in the town square."

"They say that gold ought to be worth half a billion in today's money," Nikki added.

The story had garnered our full attention. We were suckers for a good treasure hunt.

"Legend has it that the bandits buried the gold in the hills not far from Iron Horse Junction," Nikki said. "It supposedly is marked with the tombstone of Willie Jones. Believe me, a lot of people have gone looking for it, scouring every inch of Iron Horse Junction. Nobody's ever turned up with it."

"Maybe they're not using the right tools," JD said.

"Tools?"

"Ground penetrating radar. Forward-looking infrared."

"JD likes toys," I said.

"So, are you two going to talk all night, or are you going to get in the water?" Nikki asked.

32

I 'd be lying if I said my heartbeat didn't double when Sadie peeled out of that uniform. She looked damn good in it, but out of it, my God...

She wore a frilly pair of white lace panties and a bra to match. The push-up worked as intended and created a delightful valley of all-natural cleavage.

I didn't waste any time peeling out of my clothes, and we slipped into the water with the others. It was a little cool, but the hot weather had kept the water a little warmer than normal for this time of year.

There was no telling what was under the inky surface, but I was pretty sure there weren't any sharks, alligators, or prehistoric monsters. But snakes were always a reality.

The couples paired off, and Sadie and I found ourselves treading water near the stern.

"So tell me more about this gold?"

"Is that all you're interested in?" Sadie asked in a sassy tone.

"I'm not interested in the gold at all. I'm just trying to keep my mind off other things."

"And what *other things* would those be?" she asked, knowing damn good and well what was on my mind.

We stared into each other's eyes for a moment and drifted a little closer. There wasn't another thought in my brain besides our imminent collision. I leaned in, and she didn't pull away.

Game on.

I tasted her lips and pulled her close. The spark of desire burned hotter than the Texas sun.

Nikki hooted. "Woohoo! I'm going to tell Sheriff Daniels."

Sadie broke free and gave her a saucy look.

Nikki laughed. "Don't worry. Your secret's safe with me, honey."

"I know it is because I got plenty of dirt on you."

Nikki laughed. "Touché."

Sadie flung her arms around my neck and pulled herself close again. "As I was saying." She planted her plump lips on mine, and our tongues danced under the moonlight.

I believe I could get used to Texas.

We fooled around a bit, and she didn't have to wonder about my level of enthusiasm. We were both having fun, but this wasn't going to go too far. Not here, not now.

It was about midnight by the time we got back to the Buzzard's Roost.

Despite Nikki's flirtatious nature, I don't think she was going to give JD what he wanted just yet. Her friends dropped us off at the pier, and we said our goodbyes. Sadie drove us back to McAllister's ranch. I hopped out and got JD's door. He ambled inside, giving us some privacy for a moment.

Sadie climbed out of the patrol car, and I moved close.

"I guess this is goodnight," she said.

"I guess it is."

"You're never going to look at me the same way again."

"I think I will."

"You've seen what's under the uniform."

"Not all of it."

She blushed.

"But this was a good start." I paused as we stared at each other for a moment. "Want to come inside?"

"No. That would certainly lead to trouble."

"That's right, you don't associate with scoundrels."

"Apparently, I'm breaking some of my own rules," she said with a smirk. "What time do you plan on searching for Gracie tomorrow?"

"I guess it depends on what time JD's toys get here."

"How about I show up at 10?"

"Or you could just stay the night."

"I don't think Tiffany wants another houseguest."

"I don't think she'd mind."

"Blair might." Sadie lifted up on her toes and kissed me again. Her lips were soft and pillowy, and they felt just right.

All too soon, she pulled away. "Good night, Deputy."

"Good night, Deputy."

Unmistakable moans drifted across the property, interrupting the quiet moment.

It didn't take long to pinpoint the sounds of passion. They spilled from the stables.

Sadie and I exchanged a glance, then crept toward the commotion to see *who* was indulging in *what* with *whom*.

33

I t didn't come as a shock to see Cole giving it to Blair atop a hay bale. The two went at it hot and heavy. He cupped his hand over her mouth, trying to lessen the volume of the vixen's moans. But she had lost herself in the moment. There was no quieting the storm of passion. Her legs wrapped around him, and their hips collided.

We peered around the corner, watching for a moment.

The horses looked unimpressed.

Sadie and I exchanged a glance, then snuck away and left them to their business.

"I don't think that's a recent development," I said as we hurried back to the main house. "I think that's the prime motive."

"You think she killed Jim?"

"Not her. The rodeo stud."

I think Sadie was starting to share my paranoia. "What are you going to do?"

"I'm going to get proof, and you're going to nail them to the wall."

Sadie smiled.

We returned to the patrol car.

"You sure you don't want to come in for a minute?"

"If I come in for a minute, I'll be here till morning."

"That's not such a bad thing."

She gave me a look. "I'm not gonna make it that easy for you."

"I do love a challenge."

She lifted a saucy eyebrow. "Is that all I am? A challenge?"

"You're much more than that."

"We'll see."

She climbed into her patrol car, cranked up the engine, and drove away. I watched her go, then climbed the steps to the portico and pushed inside. I made my way up to the guest room in the darkness and fell into bed. The vision of Deputy Sawyer out of uniform had been burned into my retina. It was fuel for a few pleasant dreams.

In the morning, I pulled myself out of bed and stumbled down to the kitchen. Tiffany had beat me there, and she'd cooked up a nice spread. I was so used to cooking breakfast for the gang. This was an odd change of pace. "You do this every morning?"

"Well, I don't have a kitchen like this at the dorm, so I'm taking advantage of it. Besides, like I said, it soothes my restless heart at the moment. Don't be surprised if I start baking soon."

"You won't get any complaints from me."

I wasn't exactly sure how to broach the subject of the barnyard activity last night. Now wasn't the time or place.

"What are your plans for the day?" Tiffany asked.

"If you don't mind, JD and I are going to take out the boat and look for Gracie Hutchins."

Tiffany gasped. "You think...?"

I nodded and filled her in on my full theory.

JD stumbled into the kitchen a few moments later. "I think my toys are here. I just got a notification that they've been delivered, but the delivery driver couldn't get onto the property. So he left them at the gate. It's all sitting out there right now. We better grab it before somebody walks off with it."

We hustled out of the kitchen, stepped outside, and took the Porsche down to the gate. There was a ton of stuff. Heavy boxes of equipment. More than would fit in the sports car.

We opened the gate, loaded the stuff onto the property, then tried to figure out how to get it all back to the house. JD called Tiffany, and she said she'd send Cole to pick it up in his truck.

We waited with the gear for him to arrive.

"What the hell did you get?" I asked.

JD grinned. "You'll see."

Cole arrived a few moments later and helped us load the gear into the bed. We followed him back to the house, brought everything inside, and unboxed it in the living room.

34

J D had ordered Dräger re-breathers, dive masks, fins, snorkels, and a state-of-the-art underwater drone. It was a sleek white craft that looked like an alien spaceship. It had a 4K camera, two props, and a remote tether to a surface buoy that allowed for wireless operation. It was smaller than the drone we had back in Coconut Key. A slightly different feature set, but technology was advancing at a fast pace.

This stuff must have cost a small fortune.

"Planning on an adventure?" Tiffany asked as she marveled at the gear.

"Something like that," JD said.

Cole asked, "What are you gonna do with all that?"

"Find a missing girl," JD said with confidence.

Blair entered the living room and surveyed the equipment. "I always wanted to learn how to scuba dive."

"Maybe I can teach you," JD said.

"I think I'd like that."

Cole's face tensed with jealousy.

Blair took a deep breath through her nose. "Breakfast smells good. Thank you, Tiffany."

She disappeared into the kitchen, and Cole followed.

We all exchanged an awkward glance. The moment was broken by a knock at the door.

I jogged into the foyer to answer.

Sadie stood on the porch, wearing a skimpy bikini top, jean shorts, and sneakers. She had her pistol holstered for an appendix carry. A colorful beach towel dangled from her silky shoulders, and a wide-brimmed hat shaded her face. She wore oversized sunglasses. A bag full of lotion, snacks, and other goodies dangled from her arm.

"Good morning, Deputy," she said with a smile.

I soaked in her luscious form. "You look... different."

"It's my day off."

"So, you're going to search for a body with us on your day off?"

"It's technically your day off, too. Don't look at me like I'm crazy."

"I'd never look at you like that."

She smiled, and I invited her in. We joined the others in the living room. Sadie was impressed by the toys.

"Mind if I tag along?" Tiffany asked.

"Are you sure?" JD asked. "It might not be pretty if we find something."

"I can handle it," she assured. "Besides, I could use a distraction."

JD and I hauled the gear down to the dock and loaded it aboard the boat. We stocked up on snacks, bottled water, diet soda, and possibly a few beers, then headed out on the water. JD took the helm and brought the boat on plane. The air was still, and the lake like glass. A perfect day for waterskiing.

The outboards howled, and the ride was smooth.

Now was as good a time as any to update Tiffany on the situation in the stables. I hated to spread gossip, but this was more than gossip.

Tiffany growled.

"I don't want you saying anything or confronting either one of them just yet," I warned.

She huffed. "I won't." She paused, and anger swelled. "That son-of-a-bitch."

"I don't know if it's a recent development or if it's been ongoing."

"Do not take matters into your own hands," Sadie cautioned.

Tiffany composed herself and smiled. "I'll keep playing nice and pretending I'm oblivious."

"I think that's the best course of action right now." I offered a sympathetic frown. "I promise we're going to get to the bottom of this."

We pulled to the pier at the Buzzard's Roost, and Nikki greeted us on the dock with a bubbly smile. "Howdy, y'all!"

JD helped her aboard the boat, and we fueled up while we were there.

We left the Roost, and Sadie guided us to the spot that she would pick to dump a body.

Coyote Canyon Lake was a popular fishing hole. The lake had been stocked with largemouth bass and catfish. While it was possible that someone with sophisticated sonar might stumble across Gracie's body, most commercial units just didn't have the resolution. Even with the ones that did, environmental and aquatic factors made interpretation of the imaging difficult. It would be unlikely that fishermen would stumble across a submerged body unless they snagged it with a fishing line. Even then, the line would snap under the weight and wouldn't arouse much suspicion. Usually, bodies will float to the surface as decomposition gasses fill the abdomen. But a body properly weighted down could remain undetected forever.

The depth of the lake varied widely depending on rainfall and environmental conditions. But on average, the deepest part of the lake was around 200 feet. That was just within the length of the tether for the surface buoy.

We picked a spot, dropped anchor, and prepared to deploy the drone. JD connected it to his phone via Bluetooth, and we launched it in the water. The wireless app allowed him to control the camera and the drone from his phone. It was pretty sophisticated stuff, and the device had the most advanced side-scan sonar you could get in this class.

The sleek white craft plummeted into the murky depths.

We realized right away this was going to be a challenge. Visibility in the lake was 10 to 15 feet at best. We were a long way from the crystal clear waters of Coconut Key.

It could take months or years to cover every square foot of the lake bed. We were rolling the dice, and the odds weren't good.

The submersible drone made a slow descent, then JD navigated it along the silty bottom. It was a glimpse into a rarely seen world. And some of the sights were surprising.

35

The drone cruised past an algae-covered toilet, an old tire, beer bottles, and other bits of trash. Jack piloted the drone, surveying the area. We were in that spot for almost an hour, idling around. I piloted the boat while JD piloted the ROV.

An 82-foot SunTrekker yacht cruised by. It was a sleek starter yacht with a navy hull and white trim. Windswept lines and large windows. Several scantily clad beauties lounged on sun pads on the foredeck, their skin glistening with oil. I was surprised to see a vessel of that size on this lake. The girls waved, and Nikki waved back like she knew them. In a town like this, everybody knew everybody. A couple guys on the aft deck drank beer.

"Who's that?" JD asked.

"That's Rafael's boat," Nikki said.

"Who's Rafael?"

"He owns the Prancing Pony and Saddle Up."

"He's the richest guy in town," Sadie added.

"I'm not so sure about that," JD muttered.

Jack had done really well in the market. He had that kind of luck. I don't know how much money he had, but it was a lot. I hadn't done too poorly, either.

"All the shiny new squad cars we have came as a result of a generous donation from Mr. Rios," Sadie added.

"That's mighty nice of him."

"He came into town a few years ago, revamped the strip clubs, bought a couple restaurants, donated to a lot of charities. People around town either love him or hate him."

"Can't make everybody happy," JD said.

We kept searching and turned up a whole lot of nothing.

"Where else would you dump a body?" I asked Sadie.

"Well, my first choice didn't pan out. I'm not so sure you want to take my advice. I haven't dumped a lot of people in a lake, so I'm not really an expert."

I chuckled.

The smart thing to do would be to start at one end of the lake, take it sector by sector, and work our way over the entire area. But I might be close to retirement by the time we finish, and we might still be empty-handed.

I figured we should focus on the areas close to the Buzzard's Roost and spread out from there.

JD pulled up the drone, and we cruised back to the Buzzard's Roost. Fed by the Bluebonnet River, Coyote

Canyon Lake snaked through the rolling hills and high limestone cliffs, culminating in a large reservoir. Iron Horse Junction sat atop the cliffs not far from the Roost.

I tried to put myself in the head of Gracie's abductor. It was all speculation at this point. But her cell phone never pinged the tower after it reached the lake.

From the Roost, I piloted the boat through the channel toward the northwest a good way. It grew increasingly narrow as we approached the Bluebonnet River. In a small boat, the Bluebonnet was navigable for miles and miles.

There were some pretty secluded sections with high cliffs and lots of foliage. It was a perfect area for water skiing.

After we'd gone a good distance, I spun the boat around before we reached the mouth of the river. JD deployed the drone, and we cruised back toward the Buzzard's Roost, surveying the silty bottom. The visibility wasn't good at all. It was considerably more shallow in this area. The current and increased activity rustled up sediment and debris. There was a lot more trash in this area, too—lawn chairs, camping tents, swimsuits, keys. We even found a cell phone.

36

By the time we made it back to the Buzzard's Roost, we were all hungry and in need of a bathroom break. We tied up at the pier and made our way into the restaurant. It was a little after noon, and the place was packed. The hostess seated us on the outdoor deck, and we enjoyed the shade. It wasn't quite as hot as the day before, but the heatwave was still in full effect.

We chowed down and watched boaters cruise by.

Rafael Rios and his crew pulled up in a tender. They tied up at the dock, hopped out, and sauntered into the restaurant. The gentleman had a bikini-clad beauty on either arm. He was certainly living the dream.

Rafael was in his 40s with dark hair, narrow dark eyes, and a little bit of salt-and-pepper stubble. He was handsome and athletic, and I think the ladies would have pawed on him with or without his money. He was well-dressed, wearing cream shorts, a pale blue collared short-sleeve shirt, and an expensive gold watch.

He was with a couple other guys. They all flooded into the restaurant, and the hostess greeted him with a bright smile and ushered the crew to a table right away. Something told me he was a regular here and a big tipper.

They took a seat at a table on the deck not far from us.

A waitress hurried to attend to their every need.

Rafael ordered drinks and appetizers for the table. He spotted Tiffany, excused himself from his entourage, and approached. "I just wanted to express my deepest condolences. If there is anything you need, please don't hesitate to ask. The community has suffered a terrible loss."

"Thank you," Tiffany said.

"How are you holding up?"

Tiffany sighed. "As well as can be expected, I guess."

"Hang in there. It gets easier."

She smiled. "I hope so."

Rafael nodded to Deputy Sawyer.

"Good afternoon, Mr. Rios."

"Deputy."

His eyes found JD and me. "I don't believe we've met."

Sadie introduced us, and we exchanged pleasantries.

"I hope our fair city is treating you well," Rafael said with a smile.

"We're enjoying this fine Texas hospitality," I said, glossing over our initial drama with the sheriff.

"Well, allow me to extend that hospitality even further. Do you like Tex-Mex?"

"Who doesn't?"

"You must be my guest in my restaurant, the Caliente Cantina, this evening. I'll call the manager and make arrangements. Compliments of the house."

"Much obliged."

"Enjoy your stay, gentlemen. Who knows, you might like it so much here that you never want to leave."

"It has its charm."

"Indeed."

He offered his condolences once again to Tiffany, then returned to his entourage.

Another young man approached the table after Rafael left. He was early 20s with short brown hair, brown eyes, and an athletic frame. He had smooth skin and a square jaw. His eyes were focused on Tiffany as he approached. In a shy voice, he said, "Excuse me, I don't mean to interrupt. I just wanted to express my sympathies," he said to Tiffany.

"Thank you, Eli."

He hesitated a moment and looked at the floor, then back up at her. He clearly had a little crush. "If you need anything. You know how to get hold of me."

Tiffany nodded.

There was another awkward moment. "Well, enjoy your meal."

He spun around and rejoined his friends at a table across the deck.

"He's cute," Nikki said.

"He's not interested."

"Are you blind? He's more than interested. You should ask him out."

Tiffany's cheeks flushed. "I will not ask him out. If he wants to take me out, he can ask me."

"Careful, some sweet young thing will snatch him up. He's good stock."

Tiffany rolled her eyes, still blushing.

We ate and sat on the deck, letting our food digest, then headed back out on the lake and continued searching for Gracie Hutchins. I wasn't terribly optimistic, but we went through the motions. At least we had given it a shot.

We returned to the ranch in the evening, a little redder and with deeper tan lines. We were all pretty spent from the day in the sun. JD and I unloaded the dive gear and the drone and carried everything up to the back patio.

We took a moment to cool off in the living room.

"I should go home and get changed if we're going to dinner," Sadie said.

"I've got plenty of clothes you can borrow," Tiffany said. "We're about the same size."

"Are you sure?"

"No trouble at all. You can take a shower in one of the guest bathrooms. And help yourself to my makeup." Tiffany looked at Nikki. "You too."

The girls considered it.

"Come on," Tiffany urged with a smile. "Let's go raid my closet. It's time to play dress-up."

The girls followed Tiffany to her room.

JD and I got cleaned up and changed, then waited on the girls. They emerged an hour later, all done up. All things considered, it wasn't a bad turnaround, and they sure looked good.

It was the first time I'd seen Deputy Sawyer in a dress, and the vision didn't disappoint. I had no doubt the sundress would look even better on the floor.

We left the house, and Nikki rode to the restaurant with Jack. Tiffany and I hitched a ride with Deputy Sawyer.

"I've never been in the back of a patrol car before," Tiffany said.

"I'm sure you won't make it a habit," Sadie replied.

We drove to the cantina, and the hostess seated us in a large booth. The walls were painted in vibrant colors of yellow, teal, and red. Hanging lights with sombreros for shades illuminated the tables, the walls were adorned with colorful artwork, and a mariachi band played, moving about the restaurant. The smell of sizzling beef and chicken wafted through the air.

We perused the menu, but I already knew what I wanted. Beef fajitas with onions, refried beans, rice, avocado, sour cream, and pico de gallo wrapped in a flour tortilla. We started off with chips and queso, and had to indulge in a few margaritas. We finished the meal off with succulent tres leches.

It was sinful.

I was quickly reminded that Texas had the best Mexican food.

The meal was on the house, but we left the waitress a nice tip. I told her to express our gratitude to Rafael.

We left the restaurant with full bellies and headed back to the ranch. We had a full day and were ready to call it an evening. We all gathered in the living room and watched a movie on the flatscreen. I cozied up with Sadie on the couch, and Nikki nuzzled Jack. Tiffany curled up in a big leather recliner.

I hadn't seen Blair all evening.

It was around 11:00 PM when the movie ended.

"Well, I've gotta work in the morning," Sadie said. "I should probably get home."

"There are plenty of guestrooms," Tiffany said. "You're more than welcome to stay here."

"I don't want to impose."

"Nonsense. We hardly ever have any guests, and frankly, I appreciate the company right now. Keeps my mind off of things. Plus, I don't know how long I'm going to have access to this place. Better make the most of it."

"I really should get home," Sadie said.

"I got a dozen extra toothbrushes from the dentist, still in the package. I got shampoo, body wash, and everything you may need."

"You're quite the host."

Tiffany climbed out of her recliner. "Come on. I'll show you to your rooms."

She gave me a subtle wink, then led the girls upstairs. Tiffany returned a moment later, before the others. She whispered. "Am I the best wingman, or what?"

She gave me a high five.

Sadie and Nikki returned after a few moments, giggling and gossiping. Tiffany put on another movie and passed out halfway through.

I found a blanket and covered her on the recliner, then Sadie and I retired to our guest rooms. She must have gotten lost because she ended up in mine.

37

Sadie planted her full lips on mine, and we picked up right where we left off. I pulled her body against me, and her warmth radiated. Our slick tongues danced, and my pulse pounded with excitement. My hands explored the curves of her body over the top of the cotton sundress. Soon the straps fell from her shoulders, and the dainty thing fluttered to the floor, pooling at her ankles.

She wore nothing underneath.

I took a moment to soak in her beauty.

My heart stopped for an instant, then proceeded at double time. The girl took my breath away.

She helped me peel off my shirt and didn't waste any time unbuckling my pants. She dropped to her knees and saluted the captain. We tumbled around the sheets for a while, trying to be discreet about it, but I don't think we succeeded. She was a Texas girl, and she knew how to saddle up. We had our own little rodeo.

We worked ourselves up into a fevered pace, then crescendoed with a mad explosion of passion. We collapsed beside each other, sweaty and slick, heady with the remnants of margaritas.

She nuzzled close and stroked my chest. "Not a word about this to my father."

"You make it sound naughty."

"He does not need to know. You're already on his bad side. You don't want to get on his worse side."

"So, I shouldn't text him and tell him his daughter's great in the sack."

She smacked me playfully. "No. You most certainly should not do that." She paused. "Great? Just great?"

"Well, I would've said amazing, but I figured I should play it cool."

She laughed.

"If you're lucky, you might get to play again," she said, then nibbled on my ear.

I was totally up for round two.

38

The morning sun beamed through the windows. I stretched and yawned. Sadie was already up and getting dressed.

I dragged myself out of bed, pulled on some shorts and a T-shirt, then we headed down to the kitchen to see what Tiffany had whipped up for breakfast. But I didn't smell any coffee or bacon. Nothing sizzled on the grill. The kitchen was empty.

Tiffany burst through the front door, looking worried.

"What's the matter?" I asked.

"Slight problem."

I waited for a response.

"Do you know anything about cows?"

I shrugged.

"Well, we've got a dead one. I need to find out why. I hope there's not some type of disease running through the herd."

She sighed. "I don't know why I'm getting so upset about it. It's not like the ranch is mine," she muttered.

"It would have upset your father. You don't have to let go of this place just yet, or him."

She forced a smile and nodded.

"Let's take a look," I said.

Tiffany led us out of the house to a pasture where the behemoth lay, flies buzzing around the carcass.

"I didn't notice this last night, but we were pretty preoccupied," Tiffany said. "Some more than others," she added just to tease us.

Sadie blushed.

"I tried calling Dale Morris, but I can't get in touch with him."

"Have you tried Jethro?" Sadie asked.

"Do you have his number handy?"

"Yeah, I think so," Sadie said. "I'll run inside and grab my phone."

She hustled back to the house.

I looked around for the ranch hand but didn't see him. "Where's Cole?"

"I think he went into town early. This must have just happened. He would have noticed on the way out. Then again, he's been a little preoccupied lately, too."

Sadie returned and shared Jethro's contact with Tiffany.

She called the vet and explained the situation. "You think you can come out and take a look?" Tiffany listened intently for a moment. "Yes. That would be great. Thank you so much." She ended the call and told us, "He's on his way."

We went back inside, and I told Tiffany to relax. I would handle breakfast today. I grilled up a feast—ham and cheese omelets, bacon, hash browns, and waffles.

JD and Nikki joined us, as well as Blair.

Tiffany updated her.

"I'm so glad you're here to keep an eye on these kinds of things," Blair said.

Tiffany forced a smile.

We filled our bellies and waited for Jethro to arrive. The unmistakable sound of tires against gravel filtered through the windows. Jethro's old white Ford truck rumbled down the main entrance. He spotted the problem right away. He parked the truck, hopped out, ducked between the barbed wire fence, and stepped into the pasture to examine the fallen animal.

We hustled to join him.

It was almost like a crime scene. Jethro examined the beast in meticulous detail. He was in his late 50s, early 60s, with thinning light brown hair, down-turned hazel eyes, and a slim face.

He examined every inch of the creature. "Still warm. I'd say she's been dead about an hour or two. No obvious signs of trauma. No gunshots."

It was always a consideration around here. Hard as it was to believe, sometimes cows did get mistaken for deer. Occasionally, somebody got antsy and saw movement in the trees and fired first. But that was not the case here. This pasture was wide open. Of course, sometimes people took potshots from the highway just to cause mischief.

Jethro poked and prodded, pushing around the cow's abdomen, trying to feel its internal organs. He looked perplexed after feeling around for a bit, then he moved back to his truck and returned with a clear plastic glove that stretched all the way up to his shoulder. At first, I wondered what it was for.

Then I found out.

With a tube of KY jelly, he lubed up the glove and then proceeded to put it somewhere I don't think the cow would have appreciated if it was still alive. He reached up there as far as he could go, and we cringed.

"Here's your problem," Jethro said as he pulled out what looked like a brick of cocaine from the animal's rectum. It was wrapped in black plastic, but the packaging had ruptured, delivering a fatal dose of the stimulant to the poor animal.

Tiffany looked on in horror. "What is that?"

I told her.

Of course, I didn't have a field test kit, but I'd seen enough cocaine to know what it was.

"What's it doing there?" Tiffany asked.

Jethro asked, "Where did your dad get these cows?"

"I don't know," Tiffany said. "We used to raise them till they were about 600 pounds, then we brought them to market. Then my dad went completely organic and started finishing them. More money. I know, at times, he would buy them from other organic ranchers at 600 pounds and finish them."

"Well, I don't think these came from a local rancher," Jethro said.

"How did *that* get there?" Tiffany asked.

"Sometimes the cartel will use cattle to transport shipments of drugs up from South Texas," I said.

Tiffany's eyes rounded.

"They'll stuff the kilos where the sun doesn't shine or surgically put them into the abdomen."

I asked Jethro, "Have you encountered this kind of thing before?"

"Not first-hand. But I've heard stories."

"How long has that been there?"

Jethro shrugged. "Hard to say. It was lodged in there, causing a bowel obstruction."

A grave look washed over Tiffany's face. "You don't think my dad was involved with..."

"It's possible he bought the cows from somebody else, and the cartel overlooked a kilo," I said. Though it seemed unlikely. With a street value of $34,000 a kilo, I figured the cartel had a pretty good accounting of how many kilos were in a shipment.

Tiffany's eyes rounded.

I asked Blair, "Have you noticed anything unusual lately?"

With an innocent face, she said, "No. Jim handled all of this stuff. I focused on the horses."

I didn't expect to get a straight answer from her.

"I've been at school," Tiffany said. "I really don't know what's been going on around here, day to day." Her accusatory eyes shifted to Blair.

"I'm sure there's a logical explanation for this," Blair said.

"Did Jim keep detailed purchase records?" I asked. "I need to take a look at all of the recent transactions."

"I'll see what I can find," Blair said.

I wasn't holding my breath.

I addressed Tiffany, "You said your father was using Dale to treat the animals."

She nodded.

"I think we need to have a talk with him," JD said.

I agreed.

"You thinking what I'm thinking?" JD muttered to me.

I nodded.

Cole's truck turned onto the property and barreled down the dirt road toward us. He parked the truck, hopped out, and joined the gathering. "What's going on?"

I filled him in on the details, then pulled him aside. He exchanged a curious glance with Blair as I asked him if he had noticed anything strange around the ranch.

"I don't know. Honestly, my mind's kinda blown by what you're telling me. It doesn't sound like anything Jim would be involved in."

"Was Jim having any financial trouble?"

"Not that I'm aware of. He always paid me on time, and he never made mention of anything."

"And you never saw any of these cows being used for drug trafficking."

"No, sir."

"When was that cow acquired?"

"Just before Jim died. It's new to the herd."

"You know where he got it?"

He shook his head. "I went into town to get feed and run some errands. When I came back, it was here with a few others."

I wasn't sure I believed him.

Tiffany was in tears by now. "Do you think this is why my dad was killed?"

It was a definite possibility that Jim had gotten in over his head and wound up sideways with the cartel. But I tried to reassure her, "We shouldn't jump to any conclusions just yet."

"The sheriff needs to hear about this," Sadie whispered in my ear.

"Why don't you get yourself in uniform, come back here, and pick us up? Then we'll go talk to Dale Morris."

"The sheriff's gonna want you to stay out of this."

"I'm sure you can sweet talk him."

She gave me a sassy look.

40

D ale Morris lived off the highway in a red brick one-story house on a couple-acre plot of land. There were a few tall oaks on the property and a white Tundra parked out front.

We pulled up to the house in the patrol car, and I let JD out of the back. We ambled up to the front porch, and Sadie banged on the door.

There was no answer.

"He's here," Sadie muttered. "That's his truck."

Sadie banged again. "Dale. I know you're in there. Open up."

It was quite a few minutes before footsteps shuffled toward the door. Dale pulled it open with a curious look on his face. "What can I do for you, Deputy?"

"We just have a few questions for you," Sadie said. "You were taking care of Jim McAllister's cattle, right?"

Dale was a skinny guy in his early 60s with an angular nose, a thin face, deep bags under his eyes, and big ears. His hair had gone completely white on the sides, and he still had a little brown on top.

"Yes, ma'am. He may have used Jethro on occasion, but I'm not sure."

"You ever notice anything unusual when you were attending to the cattle?"

"What do you mean by unusual?"

"Like, cocaine stuffed in places where it shouldn't be," I said dryly.

His eyes rounded, and he swallowed hard. "Cocaine?"

"Yep."

A nervous laugh escaped his mouth, and he shook his head. "No. I ain't never seen cocaine in my entire life. Never heard of such a thing as cocaine in cattle."

"The cartel uses the cattle to avoid detection when they transport them up north from the border."

He hesitated a moment. "Well, I'll be. I'd never think of something like that. Then again, I ain't a drug dealer."

A thin mist of sweat formed on his brow.

"You know where Jim was getting his cattle?"

He sucked his lips and shook his head. "Afraid I don't." He paused. "Who are you again?"

"This is Deputy Wild," Sadie said. "Special Crimes."

"Special Crimes? You got a new task force?"

"Something like that."

"We think Jim McAllister may have gotten crossways with the cartel." In an ominous tone, I said, "No telling who they might come after next."

Dale swallowed hard. He knew a hell of a lot more than he was saying.

"You sure you never encountered anything unusual?" I asked again.

"I'm positive. Not to say that Jim wasn't doing something on his own. But I never saw anything. He would just call me to handle the regular care of the herd."

I stared at him for a long moment.

"These are dangerous people. If you know something, now's the time to say it."

"I'm sorry, mister, but I don't know anything about that."

"You get in touch if anything else comes to mind," Sadie said.

"Will do."

We said our goodbyes and strolled back to the patrol car. Dale closed the door, then peered out of a window and watched us go.

"He knows something," JD said.

I called Isabella and asked her to pull Dale's cell phone history.

Sadie gave me his number, and I passed it on to Isabella. Her fingers danced across the keys, and she reported back a moment later.

41

"**D**ale just called a prepaid cellular," Isabella said.

"Can you tie it to anybody?" I asked.

"That phone is off the grid. They didn't pick up. I'll dig into the call history and the location data and let you know what I find."

"Thanks. I appreciate it." I ended the call. "We spooked him, that's for sure."

"What's next?" Sadie asked. "How do we sort this out?"

"We keep putting pressure on Dale until he does something stupid." I thought for a moment, trying to put all the pieces together. "Let's say Jim was involved, and he got sideways with somebody. They took him out of the picture, but they also cut themselves out of a distribution line. Unless Blair is involved in overseeing it."

"I wouldn't put anything past Blair," Sadie said.

"You know her better than I do."

"She's always been opportunistic."

We returned to Jim's ranch, and Sadie dropped us off. She said she was going to have a talk with the sheriff.

We headed inside and caught up with Tiffany in the living room. She sobbed on the couch, curled up in the fetal position.

"Are you okay?"

She nodded. "I just don't know what to think."

"Don't. Right now, there are a lot of possibilities. Where's Blair?"

"She left. Said she was going into town to do some retail therapy. She sure knows how to spend money."

Blair had expensive tastes, and it was reflected in her wardrobe, shoes, and handbags.

"Where's Cole?"

"He's out, checking the herd, seeing if there are any other casualties."

"Do you feel like going through your father's records, trying to see if we can figure out where that cow came from?"

Tiffany nodded. She pulled herself off the couch, and we followed her into Jim's office. There was a mahogany desk with stacks of paperwork, a bookshelf, a gun case full of antiques and collectibles, and paintings of white-tailed deer on the walls.

"I don't really know where to begin," Tiffany said. "He wasn't really a computer guy. He kept everything on paper, written by hand."

"Sounds like Jim," JD said.

Tiffany started thumbing through papers on his desk.

We looked in binders on the bookshelf and turned the office upside down. We couldn't find any invoices that correlated to a recent cattle purchase, but it was hard to tell. Jim didn't keep the best records.

I called Isabella and asked her to sort through Jim's bank transactions.

I hated to admit it, but it all started to make sense. Jim had a decent size heard, but it wasn't huge. He and Cole worked the ranch. I didn't run the numbers, but in my estimation, the cattle operation wasn't pulling in enough to cover all the cars, the new mansion, and Blair's spending habits. I know Jim had done well in the market, and maybe he didn't need that much from the cattle. He'd get the agricultural discount on taxes. There were plenty of reasons to run a herd of cattle.

"Was your dad having any financial trouble?" I asked.

"Not that I know of. But I don't think he would have said anything if he was. He was a proud man. You know that." She sighed, then acknowledged the uncomfortable truth. "My dad was running drugs, wasn't he?"

"We can't say that for sure yet."

"As much as I don't like her, it wasn't Blair doing the smuggling. Running cattle takes work, and she's not about to do anything that would break a nail."

"I can't imagine this type of thing was going on during daylight hours. I'm sure they'd be recovering the drugs at night, if it was indeed happening on this property. You ever recall seeing anything?"

Tiffany shook her head. "If there was something going on, Cole would have to be involved. Nothing happened around here that he wasn't a part of. He was always right there whenever my dad needed him. He busts his ass around here. It was actually kind of endearing. I never thought he'd be hooking up with my stepmonster." She gagged.

We took Tiffany into town for lunch, or really, she took us. She drove Jim's truck, and we stopped at the Lazy Lasso.

We chowed down, kicked around theories about the case, then headed back to the ranch.

I talked to Cole again, and he maintained that he was unaware of any illicit activity. I was still waiting to hear back from Isabella about Dale's call logs.

The afternoon rolled into the evening, and Tiffany busied herself in the kitchen, cooking dinner. We enjoyed a nice meal, and it was rather quiet with just the three of us.

Blair returned after we ate with several bags from high-end boutiques. She hadn't been shopping in Snakebite, that was for sure. I figured she had driven to Austin and back.

"Evening, gentlemen," she said as she made a grand entrance.

"Good evening," I said.

"Smells good. Is there any left over for me?"

"Help yourself," Tiffany said.

"I'm starving," she said, surveying the leftover tenderloin. "I got you something. It's a really cute dress. I think you'll love it." She handed one of the bags to Tiffany. "I think you'll look so cute in it. But you look cute in everything."

Tiffany took the bag and pulled out the dress, then held it up to her form."

"What do you think?" Blair asked.

"I love it. Thank you!"

It was hard to tell if the gesture was genuine. Blair knew how to play the game. She was the ever-loving and supportive stepmother, ready to pull the rug out from underneath you.

Tiffany smiled and accepted the gift with grace. She folded the dress and put it back into the bag.

Blair stepped out of the kitchen and put the bags in her bedroom, then returned.

JD and I mulled over our options for the evening, but I didn't particularly want to leave Tiffany alone in the house with Blair and Cole on the property. I didn't trust anyone at this point.

We all watched another movie in the living room and had a leisurely evening. Halfway through the film, Blair stretched and yawned. She climbed out of her chair and said, "It's been a long day. I think I'm going to go to bed."

"I don't blame you," I said.

"Goodnight, everyone."

She left the living room and disappeared into the west wing.

JD and I called it an early night. We headed up to our guest rooms. After I brushed my teeth, I climbed into bed and tried to get some sleep, but my mind kept racing through possible scenarios. I had that terrible feeling that this thing was so convoluted we'd never get to the bottom of it.

It was a little after 2:00 AM when I heard glass breaking downstairs.

I had just dozed off for an instant, and I wasn't sure if it was a dream.

42

Tiffany had taken to locking the doors due to recent events. It would have been unthinkable a few years ago. Now, it was necessary.

I slipped out of bed and grabbed my pistol from the nightstand. I moved to the doorway and angled my weapon into the hall, clearing the area.

Pale moonlight filtered in through the window of my room and cast a glow into the hallway. Otherwise, it was dark.

The hairs on the back of my neck stood tall. Somebody else was in the house. There was no doubt about it.

It sounded like the intruder had broken a small pane of glass in the back door by the laundry room to gain access.

I crept to the end of the hallway, the barrel of my pistol leading the way. I held up at the landing and glanced down the stairs to the foyer.

Shafts of moonlight spilled in through the glass in the front door and the transom windows above.

I hovered there for a long moment, then put a cautious foot on the steps and descended to the foyer. When I hit the tile, I swept the barrel of my pistol left and right, clearing the area.

I stood at the base of the stairs, facing the door. There was a parlor to my right and a formal dining area to the left.

The two areas appeared clear.

I moved to the archway and hovered at the edge of the foyer, peering into the living room and central hallway.

Again, the space looked clear.

I angled my pistol into the hallway that led to the kitchen. Beyond, in the east wing, was the master bedroom, another guest bedroom, and a small lounge area. The laundry room was just east of the kitchen.

Moonlight filtered into the living room from large glass doors that opened to the patio.

The house was still.

The hallway to the master bedroom was dark.

Suddenly, the inky blackness was disrupted by a flash of gunfire coming from the laundry room. Bullets snapped down the corridor and echoed off the wall.

I ducked for cover in the foyer.

The thug advanced, firing into the drywall near the archway, trying to tag me through the wall.

I pulled back and slipped into the parlor.

Two sets of footsteps echoed, apart from mine—the shooter wasn't alone.

A perp advanced toward the foyer while his companion pushed into the parlor from the hallway entrance and opened fire.

We traded shots in the parlor.

My pistol hammered against my palm, and the tangy scent of gunpowder filled the air.

Bullets whizzed by, pelting the drywall and splintering the wood-paneled walls in the parlor.

It was dark, apart from the moonlight. The momentary flashes illuminated the thug's face. The ass-clown wore all black, his face covered with a balaclava.

I had no doubt the thug's companion was trying to flank me, moving into the foyer.

If anybody was asleep in the house, they were awake now. This was something you couldn't sleep through.

Most shots at short range in close quarters miss. Fine motor skills degrade under stress and adrenaline, especially if you lacked training. In combat, you sink to the level of your training. That's why it's so important.

I traded fire with the perp in the parlor, and the unmistakable thump of a bullet against flesh resonated.

An unsettling groan followed, and the thug tumbled back and hit the ground. He gasped and gurgled for breath, his chest thoroughly ventilated with bullets.

I spun around, anticipating his comrade who had entered the foyer from the living room. I opened fire as he poked his head around the corner and into the parlor. He ducked for cover, and I put a couple shots into the wall, hoping to hit him on the other side.

The thug dying on the floor gasped and gurgled.

I kept one eye on him and one eye on the entrance to the foyer.

Footsteps echoed through the living room.

The patio door flung open, and the remaining perp escaped to the patio and ran around the pool.

I advanced to the goon on the ground, kicked his weapon out of reach, and kept my pistol aimed at him. I inched toward the north door that opened into the hallway across from the kitchen and the laundry room. I angled my pistol down the hallway toward the living room, but I was pretty sure his comrade was long gone.

The gasping and gurgling stopped, and the thug bled out.

I flipped on the light.

JD stomped down the main steps. At least, I thought it was JD.

I shouted, "I'm in the parlor."

"It's me. Don't shoot," he replied, joining me shortly thereafter.

He inched into the parlor from the foyer. I told him about the other goon and his method of escape.

Jack moved back into the living room and cleared the area. He secured the patio door and returned a few moments later. He shook his head—no sign of the other thug.

He moved back into the foyer and shouted up the stairs. "Tiffany! We're okay. Stay where you are until we come and get you."

A timid "Okay" echoed back.

I knelt down by the thug and felt for a pulse in his neck.

There wasn't one.

I pulled off the balaclava and recognized him right away.

43

"Is it safe to come out?" Blair shouted from her bedroom.

"I think so," I said.

I snapped a photo of the dead thug in the parlor and texted the image to Isabella.

JD had secured Tiffany, and they joined us. We hovered over the body.

"That's Salvador," Tiffany said. "He works for Rafael."

He was part of Rafael's entourage at the lake. I figured him for some type of security at the time. Salvador was a big guy and stood about 6'2". He had a square jaw, slicked-back hair, and brown eyes.

Adrenaline spiked when Cole entered the house through the back door. I was on high alert status. He crunched over broken glass and shouted into the house, "Is everybody okay? What's going on?"

"We're in the parlor," Blair said.

Cole joined, shotgun in hand. His eyes widened when he saw the dead guy on the floor, a pool of crimson surrounding him.

"Why is Rafael Rios sending people to kill us?" I asked, knowing full well the answer.

Cole and Blair had dumb looks on their faces.

"It's time you two tell me what's really going on around here," I demanded.

"I don't know what's going on," Blair said.

"Somebody doesn't like us looking into this case," JD said.

"You think they came for you?" Blair asked.

Jack nodded.

"I think we spooked Dale, and Dale made a few phone calls," I said.

"I don't know what's going on," Blair said. "But I sure would like to."

Cole asked her if she was okay.

Blair nodded. "Just a little frazzled. That's all. Thank you."

It was clear he had feelings for her. You could see it in his eyes and hear it in his tone. Tender and compassionate.

I called Sadie and told her what had happened.

She arrived with Sheriff Donnelly, and I went over the situation with them.

Donnelly looked over the body with a tight face. "I knew you two were going to be trouble, but I didn't know you were going to be *this* much trouble."

I raised my hands innocently. "Hey, they came after us."

"Are you sure that's who they came for?"

Peyton Granger, the medical examiner, arrived. She was in her 50s with shoulder-length gray hair, elegant bone structure, and blue eyes. She had a thin frame and wore pressed wranglers and rattlesnake boots. She snapped on a pair of gloves as she approached the remains. Peyton squatted down and felt for a pulse. "Yep. He's dead, alright."

She was a no-nonsense gal—Texas through and through.

"I'll have a talk with Rafael Rios," Donnelly said.

"I'd like to be a party to that conversation," I said.

He gave me a look, but my expression told him that I wasn't taking *no* for an answer.

"Before we talk to him, we need to put pressure on Dale Morris," I said. "It's clear to me that his first call after we talked was to Rafael."

"How do you know that?"

I shrugged.

"Right. Sources."

"The stronger the case we can build against Rafael, the better. He's going to deny any involvement."

Donnelly considered it for a moment. "*We* aren't going to do anything. You two are going to hand over your weapons and stay here."

I scoffed. "Not going to happen."

Nobody defied the sheriff, and he gave me an astonished look.

"I don't work for you, remember? You can't put me on leave."

"I can take you to jail for murder and confiscate your weapon as part of the investigation."

He was just trying to be a hard-ass.

"That's a justified shooting, and you know it."

The sheriff frowned at me.

"You've got bigger problems than JD and me. And you're going to need our help."

He stared at me for a long moment. He knew I was right.

With a pained look, he said, "Alright. Let's see what Dale has to say."

Peyton and her crew bagged the remains, transferred them to a gurney, and loaded them into the back of the medical examiner's van.

"Sheriff, do you think it's safe here?" Blair asked.

"I'm beginning to think there's no place safe. Might want to go to a motel for the night."

"I'll stand watch," Cole replied.

"Thank you, Cole," Blair purred.

"I'm going to go back to my dorm," Tiffany said. "I'm not really comfortable here right now."

"I think that's a good idea," I said.

We waited for her to gather her belongings, then saw her off.

"Are you okay to drive now?" I asked.

"Believe me," Tiffany said with wide eyes. "I'm not going to sleep anytime soon."

"Call us when you get to the dorm," JD said. "Doesn't matter what time."

Tiffany nodded and climbed into her car.

We watched her drive off, then hopped in with Deputy Sawyer and followed the sheriff to Dale's property.

We gathered on the front porch, and Donnelly warned, "Let us handle this. You two can observe. You've already killed one person tonight."

"Not by choice."

Donnelly put a heavy fist against the door.

There was no response.

He banged again. "Dale! Open up!"

Again, there was nothing.

Donnelly tried the handle.

It was unlocked.

He pushed the door open with a creak. He shouted into the house again. "Dale! It's Sheriff Donnelly. Are you home?"

The lights were out. It was the wee hours of the morning. Dale's truck was parked out front.

The sheriff drew his pistol and advanced into the foyer, spotting the area with the beam of his flashlight. He fumbled for the light switch and flicked it on, then advanced into the living room. The narrow beam flashed across the area, making its way toward the hallway that led to the bedrooms.

"Shit," Donnelly grumbled.

He found another light switch.

We flowed into the house behind him.

Dale lay in the hallway with two bullets in his chest. Crimson wounds had oozed blood onto the floor, pooling around his body.

The sheriff advanced, squatted down beside him, and felt for a pulse.

Dale had long since stopped breathing.

I moved through the kitchen and checked the back door.

There were no signs of forced entry. Didn't need to be.

The back door was unlocked and ajar. I figured that's where the assassin, or assassins, had entered.

Donnelly grumbled when I returned, "That's two homicides in one night. That's never happened in this county before."

He gave me a look like it was my fault. Maybe it was.

"Somebody's cleaning up loose ends," I said.

"By the way, ballistics came back on the rifles we took from Earl and Cooter," the sheriff said. "I think it's pretty obvious at this point, but they weren't a match."

I'd pretty much written them off as suspects already.

Donnelly called Peyton and told her she had another customer.

We waited for her to arrive.

Peyton did her business, and her crew bagged the body. In a dry tone, she asked, "Are you expecting any more bodies tonight, Sheriff?"

44

R afael Rios lived in a stunning villa in the hills above the lake. The property was gated and fenced with a high perimeter wall.

The sheriff pulled his vehicle to the call box in front of the black wrought-iron gate. He buzzed the box repeatedly.

Finally, a voice crackled through the speaker. "What is it?"

"Need to have a word with Rafael," Donnelly said.

There was a long pause, then the gate opened.

The sheriff drove through, and we followed him up the asphalt driveway to the villa on the hill. The large stucco building had a coral color with a Spanish tile roof.

We piled out of the vehicles and marched to the front door. The sheriff knocked, and a moment later, an associate opened.

I recognized him from the lake as well. He had long dark hair pulled into a tight ponytail, a trimmed goatee, and a face pocked with acne scars. Muscular, but not a body-builder. He had cold eyes inset behind his low brow. He had the same build as the assailant who got away. "What can I do for you, sheriff?"

Donnelly said, "As I mentioned, Ernesto, I need a word with Rafael."

"It's a little early for a social call, isn't it?" His eyes flicked to JD and me.

"This isn't a social call," Donnelly said.

Rafael appeared in the foyer behind him. He was fully dressed in a cream linen suit. He put on a charming smile. "You're a little early for breakfast."

"Have you noticed that you're missing an employee?" Donnelly asked.

"Am I?"

"Salvador is in the morgue right now."

Rafael's eyes rounded. "Oh, no! What happened?"

"Apparently, he thought it would be a good idea to break into the McAllister residence and start shooting at people."

Rafael's jaw dropped. "I'm stunned."

"He wasn't alone, either," I said. "His companion got away before I could shoot him," I said, shifting my gaze to Ernesto.

"I don't understand," Rafael said. "Do you think he was trying to burglarize the home?"

"No," I said. "I think he was trying to kill us."

Rafael feigned confusion. "Why would he do a thing like that?"

"I think you know why."

Rafael acted bewildered. "I can't imagine. And I can assure you I thoroughly vet my employees. This is just as much a shock to me as it is to you."

I asked Ernesto, "Where have you been this morning?"

"I've been here with Mr. Rios all night."

I didn't buy it for a second. "Can anybody verify that?"

"I can," Rios said.

"You've been up all night?"

"I have terrible bouts of insomnia," he said. "I've been up since around 2:00 AM."

"What a coincidence. That's about the time the assassins showed up at the ranch."

Rafael's eyes tightened. "I'm not sure what you're getting at, Mr. Wild."

"I don't know," I said with a smug shrug. "One of your employees shows up, trying to kill us. Makes me a little suspicious."

"What my employees do on their own time is their business. Of course, I don't condone that type of activity."

"Well, I never met the guy before this evening. I can't imagine that he had that much of a problem with me or my partner."

"Perhaps he was merely attempting to burglarize the house. Though I can't fathom why. I pay my employees well." He gave a solemn pause. "I'm terribly sorry this happened to you. But I don't think I like where you're going with this."

"I don't think you're going to like it at all."

The muscles in his jaw flexed. "Again, I'm sorry for the experience you had earlier tonight. Now, if you'll excuse me, gentlemen, I'd like to *try* to go back to sleep."

"Mind if we look around?" Donnelly asked.

"Do you have a warrant, Sheriff?"

Donnelly said nothing.

"If you want to search my property, I suggest you get one."

"What have you got to hide?" I asked.

"It's the principle of the thing. The people should be secure in their persons and property." Rafael glared at the sheriff. "If that's all, Sheriff."

"Sorry for the interruption," Donnelly said.

Rios closed and dead-bolted the door.

The sheriff looked at me with a tight face. I suspected Rios wasn't a guy the sheriff liked pissing off. He dumped a lot of money into the town, and that was going to dry up. He had the money to hire the best lawyers to defend him, if need be. I'm sure he'd throw a large amount of money behind another candidate for sheriff when it came time for re-election. None of those facts were lost on Donnelly.

We huddled back at the patrol cars for a moment.

"You don't buy into his line of bullshit, do you?" I asked.

"There ain't much I can do right now," Donnelly said. "If I were you, I'd get while the getting's good. Get out of town and go back to your island. I'll handle Rios. I have a bad feeling things are about to get ugly."

"Things have been ugly for a while," I said.

"Believe me, I am not gonna let this slide. I don't care how much money he has or how much pull he has around town. If he was involved, I'm going to bring him to justice."

"There's no doubt he was involved," I said.

"You have my personal guarantee that I will get to the bottom of this. But, if like you say, somebody tried to kill you tonight, I'd take that as a sign. Count your lucky stars, and get out of Dodge."

"There is no doubt in my mind they were there to kill us," I said.

"It's gonna take a lot more than that to run us off," JD said.

"Somehow, I knew you two would say that. You boys don't have enough sense to come in out of the rain."

"I don't mind a little wet work," I said.

"Sadie, take them back to the McAllister Ranch. Try to talk some sense into them. I don't need two more people dead."

Donnelly climbed into the patrol car and cranked up the engine.

Sadie gave us a look and shrugged. We climbed into her car and followed the sheriff off the property.

"That ass-clown is not going to walk away from this," I said, trying to contain my anger.

"What are you going to do?"

"You feel like making one more stop?"

"Where?" she asked with cautious eyes.

45

I t was still dark when we knocked on Audrey's door.

It took her a while to answer.

"I'm coming. Hold your horses," she shouted through the door after a few minutes of incessant banging. Her eyes flitted between the three of us when she opened. A look of dread filled her face. "It's a little early, don't you think?"

"Dale Morris is dead," Sadie said.

Audrey gasped, and her eyes grew into saucers. "What happened?"

"He was shot twice in the chest," I said. "Assassinated."

"Assassinated? Why would anyone want to kill Dale Morris?"

"Probably for the same reason somebody tried to kill us," I said. "And the same reason they will probably come for you."

Her face went pale, and her jaw dropped. "Me?"

I was grasping at straws, but I threw a theory out to see what would stick. "Jim McAllister was using cattle shipments to traffic drugs for the cartel. I suspect he wanted out, and they didn't like that. Maybe Blair is just greedy, or maybe the cartel put pressure on her to continue the operation. Maybe she saw an opportunity. Who knows? But she came to you with a fraudulent will, promised you a lot of money, and you went along with it."

Audrey's throat tightened, and she swallowed.

"Now the operation is unraveling, and the cartel is eliminating witnesses. If I were you, I'd be worried."

"I really don't know what you're talking about," she stammered.

I stared her down for a long moment. "Tell us the truth now and agree to testify, and the DA won't bring charges. This is a one-time deal. You won't get a second chance."

I had no authority to offer such a deal, but I'm sure it could be worked out.

Audrey squirmed. "I really need to start getting ready for work."

"You know how to get in touch if you change your mind," Sadie said.

"There's nothing to change. Thanks for stopping by," she said before closing the door.

I exchanged a look with Deputy Sawyer, and we returned to the patrol car.

"You're getting comfortable offering deals," Sadie muttered as we climbed into the vehicle.

I shrugged.

"You really think they'll go after her?"

"I don't think she's even on their radar, but if we can scare her into talking, why not?"

Sadie drove us back to the ranch and pulled up to the house. She put the car into park, and the engine idled. "You guys feel safe staying here tonight?"

The sky was just beginning to lighten.

"Tonight's over," I said.

"I've got a spare bedroom."

I considered the offer. "I don't want to make you a target."

"Newsflash, I'm already a target. It's sweet of you to consider my safety, though." A slight smile tugged her full lips.

"I can tell you this. If they come again, we'll be ready," JD said.

Sadie looked at her watch. "Well, my shift will be officially starting in a few hours."

"Want breakfast?" I asked. "I'm cooking."

She considered it. "How can I turn that down?"

I smiled. "You can't."

Her phone buzzed with a call. She looked at the screen and lifted a curious eyebrow. "Would you look at that?" she said before swiping the screen. "What can I do for you, Audrey?"

46

Audrey admitted to the fraudulent will.

As I suspected, Blair brought the document, forged the other signatures, and Audrey signed off on it.

With her statement, we were able to get a warrant for Blair's arrest. When we caught up with her, she was lounging by the pool, sipping on a margarita. Sweat beaded on her oily skin, and the skimpy white bikini barely held things in place. Blair didn't seem to have a care in the world until we arrived.

I wish Tiffany would have been there to see the look on Blair's face when Sadie told her she was under arrest. "Turn around and put your hands behind your back."

Blair was speechless. Her jaw dropped, and she froze in place.

"You heard me. Get off the lounge chair slowly and put your hands behind your back."

"This is ridiculous," she said in a blustery voice.

"Tell it to the judge."

Blair glared at us. "Whatever that bitch told you, she's lying."

"Well, that's up to the courts to decide," Sadie said.

Blair didn't budge. "Can I at least put on something more appropriate?"

"We have a change of clothes for you."

In a huff, Blair climbed off the lounge chair.

Sadie slapped the cuffs around Blair's petite wrists and ratcheted them tight. Sadie escorted her through the house and out the front door. "You have the right to remain silent..."

Sadie stuffed Blair into the back of the patrol car and drove her to the station.

JD and I hopped into the Porsche and followed.

Blair was processed, printed, and put into a holding cell.

"I want to interview her," I said.

"Do I need to remind you that you don't work for the county?" Sheriff Donnelly said. "I'll handle the interview. How about you go back to the ranch, call Tiffany, and tell her that it looks like the property is going to stay in the family?"

I frowned at him. "I've got a lot of experience getting people to talk about things they don't want to talk about. And she wouldn't be in there if we hadn't kept pushing this thing."

Donnelly sucked in a tight breath. "Okay. But I'm in the room with you, and when I cut it off, that's it."

A call came in, and the dispatcher shouted to the sheriff. "We got another call complaining about Cletus. Looks like he climbed the top of the water tower buck naked again. What do you want to do about it?"

"Sadie, run out there and see if you can talk him down," Donnelly said.

"I don't know if that's something I want to see again."

He gave her a look. "I'm sure he's drunk as a skunk. I don't think he'll jump, but see if you can talk him down. He'll listen to you. I think he likes you."

"Everybody likes me," she said with a grin.

She winked at me before leaving.

Donnelly picked up on it. His suspicious eyes blazed into me, but he didn't say anything about it. "Let's go talk to your suspect."

Sheriff Donnelly led us to the interrogation room. There was a camera on a tripod in the corner, and fluorescent lights buzzed overhead. They didn't have a two-way mirror set up. There was nothing high-tech about it. We took a seat across the table from Blair, and she surveyed us with curious eyes.

"I welcomed you as guests in my home, fed you, treated you right, and this is how you repay my hospitality? By convincing Audrey to make false allegations."

"Cut the crap, Blair," I said. "We know what you did, and handwriting analysis between the two wills is going to prove that Jim didn't sign the revised document. Combined with Audrey's testimony, you're going to go away for a long time.

But the sheriff is willing to give you an opportunity to save your ass."

He looked at me and lifted a curious brow. He'd made no such promise.

"You tell us everything you know about Rafael Rios and his operation, and you might not spend the next 30 years behind bars on a fraud charge."

I didn't know what the penalties were in Texas. I was shooting from the hip.

"It's a first-degree felony," Sheriff Donnelly said, backing up my threat. "The value of that property is well over $300,000. I don't know how they do things in Florida, but in Texas, you could be looking at up to 99 years."

"Something tells me you're not gonna look quite as good in that bikini by the time you get out," I said.

Blair sneered at me.

47

"I want an attorney," Blair declared, puffing up.

That was the end of the interview, technically.

"Rafael had Jim murdered," I said. "He tried to have us killed, and Dale Morris is dead. Do you really think you're safe? It seems to me that Rafael is extremely paranoid."

Fear bathed her eyes.

"Now, I don't want to speak for the sheriff, but I think he might offer you an opportunity to walk away if you come clean."

Donnelly gave me the side-eye.

I was definitely writing checks I couldn't cash.

There was a long moment of silence.

Blair looked at the sheriff. "Is that true?"

He considered it for a moment. "Tell me what you know. If it's enough to put Rafael Rios behind bars, I'm willing to forget about this little incident. Provided that you move out of that house, take nothing from the estate, and find yourself another town to call home."

Blair considered the offer for a moment.

I was impressed. The sheriff was finally starting to work with us.

"And you can keep me safe in the meantime?" she asked.

"I'll keep you safe," the sheriff assured. "Nobody's gonna hurt you in here."

"To be perfectly honest, I had no choice in the matter."

I stifled an eye-roll.

Blair continued. "I don't know how Jim first got involved with Rafael. I know he was having a little financial trouble."

"What kind of trouble?" I asked.

"Jim thought he was invincible. He made a ton of money in the market, then got overconfident. Things kept going up. I told him he needed to diversify. But he didn't listen. He started chasing these speculative investments. The next thing you know, everything was gone." She frowned. "He thought it was going to be a short-term deal—move a few hundred head of cattle, let them ship their product, and collect the money."

"But he wanted out," I said.

Blair nodded. "You know Jim. He wasn't a bad man. I think it weighed heavily on his conscience. The money is nice. Sure. It's easy when you don't have to see the consequences. But when Grayson overdosed last month, I think that really hit home with him. The boy was only 16. Had a promising future. Great quarterback. He was on the path to a scholarship. Who knows?" She sighed. "It wasn't long after that when Jim turned up dead. I had my suspicions, and that was confirmed when Rafael's people told me that I would have to continue with their agreement. You have to believe me. I had no choice but to forge that will and control the property. I was really looking out for Tiffany," she said, trying to sound virtuous. "I told her she could stay as long as she wanted. If she would have inherited the ranch, they would have just put the same pressure on her. I just couldn't bear to see that happen."

Blair was good about making herself appear like the victim. She tried to sound sympathetic and altruistic. I think most of what she said was true, but she sure painted herself in a good light. Blair was definitely no saint, but I hoped her statement would be enough to get a warrant for Rafael's arrest.

She made a sworn affidavit, and we had her statement on video. In the hall outside of the interrogation room, Donnelly told us that he would take the information to the judge and keep us posted.

"We'd really like to be involved in the arrest," I said.

Donnelly scoffed. "There's nothing more for you to do. My department will handle it from here. You keep forgetting you're not peace officers in this state."

"You could always deputize us," I said with a smile. "You need all the help you can get. What have you got? Six patrol officers total, including yourself."

Donnelly frowned. He knew I was right.

48

JD and I drove back to the ranch and waited for the sheriff's call. I didn't know how long it would take to get a warrant in this town, but I couldn't imagine it would take too long.

Cole was in a pasture near the house when we pulled up. He hurried to greet us as we hopped out of the Porsche. His face was tense with concern. "Have you seen Blair?"

"Blair is in jail," I said, trying not to revel in the phrase.

His eyes rounded, and his jaw dropped. "What for?"

I told him the story. "We need to have a little talk. How much do you know? The time for games is over."

"Look, I just work the cattle, take care of the property, do whatever needs to be done. I didn't know for certain what was really going on, but there was something funny. Dale Morris would come out here in the middle of the night, along with Rafael and his boys. It didn't take a rocket scientist to figure out what was going on, but I wanted no part of it. I kept my head down and minded my own business."

"And slept with Jim's wife."

A guilty frown tugged his face, and his eyes fell to the dirt, embarrassed. "I knew what was going on, but what was I supposed to do? Turn him in? I need this job, and Jim was like a father to me."

"You keep saying that, but that didn't stop you from having your fun with Blair."

"I feel really bad about that. Honest, I do. But that girl's got a hold on me. She's got something. Hell, you've seen her. I feel really ashamed. But I can't help it. I love her." He frowned. "I guess you're gonna tell the sheriff now, ain't you?" He exhaled. "I don't blame you. I deserve it. I deserve everything I get."

I almost felt sorry for the kid. Blair certainly had a talent for making men do silly things.

"It's not really up to me," I said. "But I'm sure, if you're honest with the sheriff and agree to testify to everything you saw, you might be able to walk away from all this."

He nodded. "I'll do whatever it takes. I want to make this right. It's been eating me up inside."

His torment seemed genuine. Then again, he could have been a hell of an actor.

JD called Tiffany and told her the good news that the ranch was hers. I called the sheriff and let him know he had another witness willing to testify.

"I'll handle Cole," Donnelly said. "You sit tight. I'll be in touch as soon as I hear from the judge."

I considered the possibility that Cole might hop into his truck, take off, and never return to Mesquite County. But he went back to the field and resumed his work.

JD and I stepped inside and made sandwiches in the kitchen.

Cole had temporarily fixed the back door, taping a piece of cardboard where the windowpane once was. The shards of glass on the floor had been cleaned.

JD and I hurried up and waited. We both paced around, antsy. I wanted to see Rafael Rios behind bars as soon as possible.

The afternoon rolled into the evening, which gave way to night.

I was beginning to think the sheriff had stood us up. I called Sadie, but she didn't pick up. It went to voicemail, and I left a message, telling her we were back at the ranch and waiting to hear from her father.

It was a little after 10:00 PM when the sheriff buzzed with a call. "I'm heading your way with a few deputies. You boys ready?"

"Been ready all day."

"These things take time."

"Where's Sadie? I tried to call, but she didn't pick up."

"She went home and went to bed. If you hadn't noticed, it's been a long day."

I couldn't disagree.

"I should be at the McAllister ranch shortly. Don't make me regret deputizing you two."

I ended the call and slipped the phone back into my pocket with a grin. I told JD we were on, and we hustled outside to meet the sheriff.

He pulled onto the property, followed by another unit. The two squad cars pulled around by the house.

The sheriff and his deputies hopped out and approached us. "You remember Wainwright and Pritchard."

They were the two assholes that had arrested us outside of the Rattlesnake Saloon.

We shook their hands and let bygones be bygones.

"So, what's the plan?" I asked.

"Actually, there's been a change of plans," the sheriff said.

The two deputies drew their weapons and took aim at us.

"On the ground! Now!"

JD and I looked bewildered, caught off guard.

We raised our hands slowly and complied.

The two deputies pounced and slapped the cuffs around our wrists, ratcheting them tight.

"Want to tell me what this is about?" I asked. "I thought we were past this kind of thing."

49

The deputies had stuffed us into the back of the sheriff's patrol car. He drove down a dark highway, glancing at me occasionally in the rearview. He looked troubled, but not as troubled as we were.

"I'm going to tell it to you like it is," the sheriff said. "Rafael and his goons have Sadie."

That hung there for a moment, and my stomach tightened.

"They've informed me that if I don't hand you boys over to them, they'll kill her."

That sense of dread in my stomach intensified. There were no door handles on the inside of the backseat of the patrol car, and a shield of bulletproof plexiglass separated us from the sheriff.

"Do you know if she's even still alive?" I asked. "Did you get proof of life?"

I could tell by his expression he didn't. He just frowned at me in the rearview.

"How many hostage situations have you dealt with?"

"One. Jedediah got into it with his live-in girlfriend, and he threatened to kill her if we did leave the property."

"How did that turn out?"

"That ended in a murder-suicide about 10 years ago. That was the last time we had a big kerfuffle around these parts."

The sheriff turned off the highway and barreled down a narrow road, winding up through the hills. The deputies followed behind, their headlights catching the rearview now and then.

"So, how do you see this panning out?" I asked.

"I'm going to hand you two over and get my daughter back. Then things are going to go back to normal around here."

"You've known about Rafael and his operation all along," I said.

"When you get to be my age, there are some things you just come to accept. Things change, and sometimes you can't do a damn thing about it." He paused, and his hard eyes stared at me in the rearview. "I don't think you really know who you're dealing with. Rafael and his boys came into town and didn't give anyone much of a choice. He's ruthless, and with a phone call, he can have an army of cartel soldiers here to take care of any problem. Now, I could play ball and continue living a comfortable life, or I could go after him with all the piss and vinegar of a young man and watch him ruin my life. You have to understand, I'll do anything to protect my family. It's not that I totally dislike you boys. You have some redeeming qualities. But I have no choice here. I'm not gonna let him kill Sadie."

"Do you really think he's going to let her go, and things will just *go back to normal*?"

"Nobody likes change, Mr. Wild. He knows what to expect from me and my deputies. If he gets rid of me, he's gotta bring someone else in and wonder about their loyalty. Now I told you when you first got to town that you should turn around and go home. I tried to save you a lot of heartache. You didn't listen."

"We're a little stubborn that way," I said. "How much does Sadie know?"

"Until today, she didn't know anything." He took a breath, then exhaled. "She's a lot like you. An idealist. But I think, in time, she'll understand the choice that I made."

I struggled with the cuffs, but they were too tight to squeeze my hands through. I didn't have a paperclip or a bobby pin in my pocket. There was nothing to shim the cuffs with. Nothing to pick the lock.

I exchanged a subtle glance with JD to see what kind of progress he was making.

He wasn't making any.

We crossed the lake and snaked our way up toward Iron Horse Junction.

Time was running out.

50

The sheriff turned onto a dirt road, and gravel popped and pinged in the wheel wells. The car kicked up a trail of dust, illuminated by the squad car behind us.

We arrived at the top of the plateau, not far from the sheer cliffs that plunged to the lake below. The stars flickered overhead, and the crescent moon presided over our impending demise.

A black SUV sat at the top of the plateau, its lights on.

The sheriff pulled in front of it and put the car into park. He hopped out, closed the door, and walked in front of the patrol car. There were about 20 yards between his car and the SUV.

The sheriff shouted, "I want to see my daughter."

Rafael hopped out of the passenger seat, and Ernesto climbed out from behind the wheel. He moved to the back seat, opened the door, and dragged Sadie out. She was gagged, and her wrists were bound behind her back. She looked unharmed. Pissed off but unharmed.

Another goon emerged that had been sitting in the back-seat, keeping an eye on her. There were three of them total.

Rafael moved in front of the SUV.

"Let her go," the sheriff commanded.

"Relax, Sheriff," Rafael said. "She is unharmed and in perfect health. You'll get her back without a scratch if you do as I say."

"I've done everything you've asked. The Florida deputies are in the back of my car."

"I see that. Thank you." Rafael took a deep breath. "This would have been much simpler if you ran them off sooner."

"I tried."

"You didn't try hard enough."

They stared each other down for a moment.

Ernesto held onto Sadie's arm, a gun jammed in her rib cage.

Deputies Wainwright and Pritchard exited their vehicles and hung back.

"Bring the troublemakers to me," Rafael commanded.

Sheriff Donnelly glanced back at his deputies and nodded.

They moved to the squad car, opened either door, pulled us out of the vehicle, and marched us toward the sheriff.

"I brought you what you wanted. Let Sadie go."

"What's the matter, Sheriff? Don't you trust me?"

Donnelly bit his tongue.

"You just need to do one thing for me, and Sadie is yours, and everything goes back to normal."

"What's that?"

"I require absolute loyalty. The way things have been going lately, I'm getting a little concerned. I need you to demonstrate that loyalty."

I knew where this was going, and it wasn't good.

"I brought some shovels. Shoot them and bury them in the hills. I suppose, if you're inclined, you could weigh the bodies down and dump them in the lake. It's really up to you. As long as they don't get found. And if they do get found, the investigation will go nowhere."

The sheriff's jaw tightened.

Sadie looked at me with terrified eyes.

"It's getting late, Sheriff," Rafael warned.

Donnelly took a deep breath and drew his pistol. "On your knees, boys."

The two deputies shoved us to the ground.

Sadie screamed through the gag.

With our knees in the dirt, the sheriff put his pistol to the back of my head.

51

I was bathed in headlight beams, kneeling in the dirt as my heart thumped. Mists of sweat glistened my skin. I wasn't exactly sure how we were going to get out of this one.

It was probably only a fraction of a second, but it seemed like an eternity. All the moments from birth to death condensed in a millisecond. I'd visited the other side once before and been close many times since, but it still was a journey I wasn't ready to take. I had plenty left to do.

The air was still, and the howl of a distant coyote broke the silence.

The sheriff gripped the pistol tight.

JD had managed to slip his wallet from his pocket when we were in the patrol car. In it, he had a small lock-picking kit with a rake and a tension wrench. The tension wrench was just the right size to slip into the keyhole of the handcuffs. In all the commotion, he'd been working the lock without anyone noticing.

At the last second, Donnelly swung his pistol away from my head and took aim at Rafael. He squeezed the trigger, and muzzle flash flickered from the barrel. The bullet rocketed toward the scumbag, pelting him in the chest.

Geysers of crimson spewed, and Rafael tumbled to the ground in front of the SUV.

Rafael's goons didn't waste any time opening fire at Sheriff Donnelly.

He had essentially committed suicide to save us.

Donnelly twitched and convulsed with the bullet hits. He managed to get off a few shots before he hit the ground, riddled with sucking chest wounds.

JD's arms swung free, and we scampered out of the line of fire.

Donnelly's corrupt deputies picked the right side and opened fire at the cartel thugs.

Bullets crisscrossed the night, and gun smoke wafted from barrels, backlit by the headlight beams.

Metal popped and pinged as stray bullets hit quarter panels and shattered headlights.

Sadie took cover behind Rafael's SUV while the thugs went toe-to-toe with the deputies.

Both of them went down in a blaze of gunfire.

Something told me this would be historically known as the *Shoot out at Iron Horse Junction.*

The last remaining cartel thug, Ernesto, had taken a shot to the abdomen. He'd emptied his magazine in the skirmish with the deputies. He climbed behind the wheel of the SUV and pulled the door shut. He cranked up the engine and put it into gear.

From a distance, more gunfire erupted. A bullet snapped through the air, blasting the windshield, webbing it with cracks as Ernesto floored the SUV.

JD fumbled with my cuffs, and my hands swung free.

Another shot rifled through the night.

I spotted muzzle flash in the distance from the high ground.

Ernesto slumped behind the wheel, and his body tugged the wheel to the side. The SUV banked around and barreled straight for us, the headlights blinding.

I went one way, and JD went the other. Unfortunately, the way I went was straight off the cliff. It was the only way to go.

I plummeted toward the lake below, the black SUV plunging alongside me.

The wind whistled through my ears as I careened toward the surface of the water. I had no idea how deep it was here.

I hoped it was deep enough.

I splashed through the surface, plunging into the murky depths, and found the bottom.

My bones didn't break, and my ligaments didn't snap. I'd gotten lucky, to say the least.

The SUV splashed into the water, headlights first.

The amount of air inside the truck kept it bobbing at the surface for a moment, the headlights illuminating the silty bottom.

I couldn't believe my eyes.

There, in the shafts of light, was the body of Gracie Hutchins tied to a Danforth anchor. The beam illuminated her corpse like a ray of light from the heavens. An instant later, the lights flickered and shorted out.

I swam to the surface and sucked in a breath of air. I slung the water from my hair and paddled to the sheer cliff face.

JD's voice echoed from above. "You alive down there?"

52

I swam along the cliff until I found a place to come ashore, then took a trail up to the top of the plateau. My shoes squished and squeaked as I climbed to the top.

By the time I arrived at Iron Horse Junction, first responders had arrived. Red and blue lights painted the area with swatches of color. EMTs and paramedics were on the scene, and Peyton Granger had arrived.

Sadie was dazed but unharmed. Her eyes were red and puffy from tears.

Sheriff Donnelly and his two deputies were dead. Rios and his operation were no more.

I put a comforting arm around Sadie and tried to console her.

She hugged me tight.

Sadie had a lot to process and it would take a long time to put it all in perspective.

I'd been trying to figure out who shot Ernesto when Cole approached. He ambled through the chaos and found us.

"Was that you?" I asked.

He nodded. "I saw you leave with the sheriff, and I followed you up here. I had a bad feeling about it."

"Nice shooting," I said.

"I don't know if it makes anything right, but..." He frowned and shook his head. "I should have gotten involved sooner. Maybe the sheriff would still be alive." He looked at Sadie. "I'm really sorry about your dad."

She responded with a grim nod.

In the morning, we gathered the dive gear, and along with the medical examiner, recovered Gracie's body.

I had a difficult phone call to make to Maddie. The news was devastating, but it didn't come as a surprise.

In the afternoon, JD and I caught Happy Hour at Buzzard's Roost. After all we'd been through, we figured we deserved a little break.

We took a seat at the bar, ordered our usual beverage, and perused the menu. JD and I had beef brisket sliders with pickles and onions, and a side of spicy sweet potato fries.

News had spread across town of the events at Iron Horse Junction and the discovery of Gracie Hutchins. Whispers of gossip caught my ear from time to time.

The old man we were in the drunk tank with wandered to the bar and took a seat next to us.

The bartender gave him an annoyed look. "Emmett, what did I tell you?"

Emmett shrugged. "I don't recall. I'm sure you've told me a lot of things."

Emmett had a bulbous nose, a scratchy voice, big ears, and sun-worn skin. His lips were thin, and his jaw narrow. Scraggly gray hair sprouted from his skull, and his clothes were tattered and dirty. He might have been wearing the same clothes from the drunk tank, but I think he washed them in the lake. He was ripe but didn't smell near as bad as he did in the drunk tank.

"I ain't serving you no more."

"That's downright un-American."

"The last time you was in here, you didn't have any money. Then you wandered out and passed out on somebody's boat and pissed yourself. Wasn't the first time, either. I had to call the sheriff."

"Well, the sheriff ain't around no more. And you didn't *have* to call him."

"You been sleeping on someone's boat damn near every night for the past month. And I told you at least a dozen times you can't do that. I get tired of running you off."

"No harm, no foul."

"Somebody took a dump in Bobby Joe's wake boat."

"Wasn't me."

"Excuse me," I said. "You've been sleeping out in the marina every night for the last couple weeks?"

Emmett scowled at me. "What's it to you?"

"Damn right he has," the bartender said. "He's a nuisance."

"I am not," he protested. The old man's eyes narrowed at us. "I know you two."

"You remember seeing Gracie Hutchins about two weeks ago? It would have been late at night. Between 1:00 and 2:00 AM. The bar was closed.

He thought for a moment. "Yeah, I seen her. Two weeks ago, Monday. She got on a boat with two guys."

He had my curiosity. "You sure about that?"

"I remember I woke up and had to piss something fierce. I did my business in the bushes. When I got back to the dock, she was cruising off with those two fellas."

Emmett wasn't the most reliable witness at this point, but he was the only lead we had.

"You know she's been missing, right?"

"Hadn't heard."

"She was found dead," I said.

"Nobody told me."

"Who were the two guys?"

He thought about it for a moment. "Buy me a round or two, and I might think about telling you."

I nodded to the bartender. "Put whatever he wants on my tab."

"You gonna be responsible for him when he pisses himself and passes out?"

"You're not going to serve him *that* many."

The bartender reluctantly poured Emmett a drink and slid it across the counter.

Emmett lifted the glass with a smile. "Much obliged."

He downed it in an instant, then finished with a refreshing gasp.

"You were saying?"

"Hit me again, slim," Emmett said.

The bartender complied, though he was clearly annoyed.

Emmett guzzled the whiskey.

"Start talking," I said.

53

"She got on a boat with Dusty and Buck," Emmett said. "If you ask me, she was a little young to be hanging out with them, drinking beer. But who am I to judge?"

My face tightened, and I exchanged a glance with JD.

"Nikki isn't going to like that," Jack said.

I confirmed with Emmett. "You're 100% certain about that."

"I saw what I saw."

I called Sadie and updated her. With Emmett's statement, she was able to get a warrant.

Jack called Nikki. "Do you know where Dusty is?"

"He's here at the house with Buck. Why? What did he do this time?"

"Nothing. Just curious."

"I was about to go to work, but I believe you could twist my arm into playing hooky. Besides, I don't know how much longer that place is gonna be in business now that you killed my boss."

"I didn't kill your boss, Sheriff Donnelly did."

"Well, I'm not sure what's gonna happen to the club." She sighed. "I was kinda tired of that job anyway."

"Do me a favor," Jack said. "How about you leave the house and come down here to the Buzzard's Roost? I'll leave a tab open. I've gotta run a few errands, but I'll be back. Don't worry about going to work tonight."

The smile in Nikki's voice was clear. "I believe I can do that. It's usually a slow night at the club anyway," she teased.

Jack ended the call.

I said, "You think she's gonna be mad when she finds out you're going to arrest her brother?"

"We'll see, won't we?" JD said. "I just want her out of the house when we do it. Dusty is unpredictable."

We met up with Deputy Sawyer, and the three of us headed to Dusty's place. We pulled onto the property in the patrol car.

Sadie and I took the front door, and JD snuck around to the back. We stepped to the porch, and Sadie banged a hard fist. "Mesquite County! Open up! We have a warrant."

There was no response.

Noise from the TV filtered down the hallway and through the door.

Sadie shouted again. "Dusty, don't make me break down this door!"

Muffled voices rumbled inside.

I heaved a battering ram against the door, and it flung open. The jamb splintered, and the door handle put a hole in the sheetrock when it smacked the wall.

Sadie covered the foyer.

I dropped the ram and advanced into the house with my weapon drawn, and Sadie followed.

The morons had tried to escape through the back door, but Jack was there to greet them. Dusty spotted him through the window, and the dipshits turned around and hustled back through the kitchen, into the living room to find us.

Jack kicked the door, trying to break it down.

Dusty gripped a Mossberg pistol grip shotgun.

"On the ground! Now!" I commanded, my weapon aimed at his chest.

Buck's nervous eyes flicked between us.

"You got no right to be in my home?" Dusty barked.

"We got a warrant, Dusty," Sadie shouted.

Jack breached the back door and advanced.

"You're surrounded, Dusty. Put the shotgun down."

JD held up at the entrance to the kitchen, taking cover around the corner, his weapon aimed at Dusty's back.

I made sure to keep him out of my sight picture. "Put the shotgun down, Dusty."

He was looking at kidnapping, murder, and a host of other charges. It was a desperate situation. Sometimes people do desperate things. I hoped he wouldn't take the easy way out.

There was a tense moment as his eyes darted between me and Sadie.

Then he set the shotgun on the tile in the kitchen and raised his hands.

"Move away from the weapon!" I commanded. "Both of you. On the ground. Hands behind your head. Interlock your fingers."

They complied.

JD and Deputy Sawyer rushed in and slapped the cuffs around their wrists. They yanked the perps to their feet and escorted them out of the house.

Sadie began, "You have the right to remain silent..."

We stuffed them into the back of the patrol car, then JD and I took a look around. We found Gracie's bike in the garage. The whole thing really hit home when I found it. Made it real.

I took photos, then stuffed the bike into the trunk of the patrol car.

JD said he'd stay behind and break the news to Nikki.

"She might shoot you," I teased.

"She wouldn't do that." He called her cell phone. "Hey. Change of plans. I need you to meet me at your house. We need to have a little talk."

"Good luck," I said, cringing.

I climbed into the patrol car with Sadie, and we took the perps back to the Sheriff's Office. They were processed, printed, and put into a holding cell.

I figured Buck was the weaker of the two and chose to interview him first.

It didn't take long in the tiny interrogation room before he admitted the truth. His world had collapsed. "It wasn't my idea. I swear. I didn't know what was going to happen. I thought we were just going to give her a ride home. Dusty wanted to take her to the lake. She seemed into it."

"She was 14, Buck."

"She looked older."

I wanted to strangle the guy.

"Keep going," Sadie said.

"We took her out on the boat and started drinking, then Dusty started making moves. She wasn't having it."

My jaw tightened.

Buck hung his head in shame. "I told him it wasn't right."

He went on to detail the horrific things that were done to that young girl.

I think Buck thought he was going to walk away from this whole thing and pin it all on Dusty. But he admitted enough that he was going away for a long time. I figured both those boys were headed for a lethal injection. But the prosecution needed a witness, and Buck was more than willing to comply.

After we wrapped up at the station, I called JD. "Are you still alive?"

"Barely. But we got things worked out. Of course, she needs two new doors. In the meantime, you don't think Tiffany would mind if she stayed at the ranch."

I laughed. "I'm sure that'll be fine."

JD had a certain amount of charm. Only he could arrest a girl's brother and stay on her good side. Then again, Dusty was a pure scumbag.

I ended the call and told him I'd see him back at the ranch later.

Sadie approached. "I don't know what to say. This town owes you a debt of gratitude. You brought down the cartel, and you brought two ruthless predators to justice."

"Yeah, but it came at a heavy cost. I can't help thinking if we never came to town..."

"If you had never come to town, my father might still be alive. That much is true. But how long would it have been before he got sideways with Rafael and ended up just like Jim McAllister?" Her eyes brimmed. "My father was a grown man. He made his own choices. In the end, he..."

"He saved our asses. And that's the way he needs to be remembered."

She nodded and wiped the mist away from her eyes.

"What's next for you?" I asked.

"I guess I'll be taking over his duties. You know, I'm gonna need a few good deputies. If you feel like sticking around, you've got a job."

I smiled. "Something to consider."

Snakebite had its qualities.

In the morning, JD and I took Tiffany's boat for one last trip out on the lake. We loaded the dive gear aboard and went back to the spot where we had found Gracie Hutchins.

I'd noticed something else at the bottom of the lake when we pulled Gracie Hutchins out.

The tombstone of Willie Jones.

The Danforth anchor that had kept Gracie's body pinned to the bottom of the lake rested atop the stone tablet. When I had removed the anchor, it scratched away some of the sediment, revealing the tombstone. I brushed the rest clean to get a look at the name carved into the tablet.

This wasn't the final resting place of Willie Jones. It was a marker of the buried treasure. The gold stolen from the train wasn't buried atop Iron Horse Junction. It was at the bottom of it.

Finding the lost treasure came with its own problems.

There were several entities that might have a claim to it. The lake was public land, and the state could claim ownership. Of course, there was the railroad company, the insurance company that paid the claim on the theft, and the original owners of the gold. A permit for excavation was likely necessary.

Of course, we could just keep our dumb mouths shut about the whole thing.

54

As much as Snakebite and Sadie had grown on me, it was time to get back to Coconut Key. JD and I said our goodbyes, packed our bags, and hopped into the Porsche.

We'd set up a scholarship fund for Maddie, and helped her get an apartment so she could get away from Wade.

Tiffany finally called Eli and asked him out.

JD and I left town just the way we came. I was relatively sure we wouldn't run into any sheriff's deputies on the highway out of town, and Jack drove back to Austin just as fast as the car would go. Wild Fury was scheduled to play at a club on 6th Street.

My phone buzzed with a call from an unknown number. I hated answering those calls, but I swiped the screen anyway. "Hello?"

"Tyson," a woman cried.

"Madison?" I asked with confusion. I hadn't heard from my sister in years.

She sounded a wreck. Through tears, she bawled, "I need your help."

Ready for more?

The adventure continues with Wild Alpine!

Join my newsletter and find out what happens next!

AUTHOR'S NOTE

Thanks for taking this incredible journey with me. I'm having such a blast writing about Tyson and JD, and I've got plenty more adventures to come. I hope you'll stick around for the wild ride.

Thanks for all the great reviews and kind words!

If you liked this book, let me know with a review on Amazon.

Thanks for reading!

—*Tripp*

TYSON WILD

Wild Ocean

Wild Justice

Wild Rivera

Wild Tide

Wild Rain

Wild Captive

Wild Killer

Wild Honor

Wild Gold

Wild Case

Wild Crown

Wild Break

Wild Fury

Wild Surge

Wild Impact

Wild L.A.

Wild High

Wild Abyss

Wild Life

Wild Spirit

Wild Thunder

Wild Season

Wild Rage

Wild Heart

Wild Spring

Wild Outlaw

Wild Revenge

Wild Secret

Wild Envy

Wild Surf

Wild Venom

Wild Island

Wild Demon

Wild Blue

Wild Lights

Wild Target

Wild Jewel

Wild Greed

Wild Sky

Wild Storm

Wild Bay

Wild Chaos

Wild Cruise

Wild Catch

Wild Encounter

Wild Blood

Wild Vice

Wild Winter

Wild Malice

Wild Fire

Wild Deceit

Wild Massacre

Wild Illusion

Wild Mermaid

Wild Star

Wild Skin

Wild Prodigy

Wild Sport

Wild Hex

Wild West

Wild Alpine

Wild...

CONNECT WITH ME

I'm just a geek who loves to write. Follow me on Facebook.

www.trippellis.com

Made in the USA
Las Vegas, NV
13 December 2023

82718145R00163